#Delete

New York Times, USA Today & Wall Street Journal Bestselling Author

Sandi Lynn

Sandi Lynn

#Delete

Copyright © 2017 Sandi Lynn Romance, LLC

All rights reserved. No part of this publication may be reproduced, distributed, or transmitted in any form or by any means, including photocopying, recording, or other electronic or mechanical methods without the prior written permission of the publisher.
This is a work of fiction. Names, characters, places and incidents are the products of the authors imagination or are used fictitiously. Any resemblance to actual events, locales, or persons, living or dead, is entirely coincidental.

Photo & Cover Design by: Sara Eirew @ Sara Eirew Photography

Editing by B.Z. Hercules

Table of Contents

Chapter One 5
Chapter Two 11
Chapter Three 17
Chapter Four 20
Chapter Five 27
Chapter Six 34
Chapter Seven 43
Chapter Eight 52
Chapter Nine 60
Chapter Ten 66
Chapter Eleven 72
Chapter Twelve 78
Chapter Thirteen 85
Chapter Fourteen 92
Chapter Fifteen 95
Chapter Sixteen 100
Chapter Seventeen 106
Chapter Eighteen 113
Chapter Nineteen 120
Chapter Twenty 124
Chapter Twenty-One 132
Chapter Twenty-Two 138
Chapter Twenty-Three 144
Chapter Twenty-Four 151
Chapter Twenty-Five 157
Chapter Twenty-Six 165

Chapter Twenty-Seven 169
Chapter Twenty-Eight 177
Chapter Twenty-Nine 186
Chapter Thirty 192
Chapter Thirty-One 198
Chapter Thirty-Two 204
Chapter Thirty-Three 208
Chapter Thirty-Four 215
Chapter Thirty-Five 222
Chapter Thirty-Six 232
Chapter Thirty-Seven 237
Chapter Thirty-Eight 242
Chapter Thirty-Nine 248
Chapter Forty 253
Chapter Forty-One 258
Chapter Forty-Two 260
Chapter Forty-Three 265
Chapter Forty-Four 271
Chapter Forty-Five 275
Chapter Forty-Six 281
Chapter Forty-Seven 287
Books by Sandi Lynn 293
About the Author 295

Chapter One

Eloise

Men. They all come from the big genetic whirlpool of douchebag central and their brains are all wired the same when it comes to women. More than half of them don't even have life figured out, and the ones that do carry around baggage that is so over-packed the airlines would make a fortune off them. Do I sound bitter? Maybe I am. No, I know I am because growing up, the only thing I ever wanted was a relationship like the one my parents had. They'd been married twenty-seven years and were as in love with each other as the first day they met. They were a mirror for what a relationship should be. But as I found out, starting in my teenage years through my young adult life, my father was a rare find. One, who by some fate, escaped from the whirlpool of douchebag central.

Jerry and Anna's relationship wasn't perfect by any means. I mean, come on, is any relationship ever perfect? Is perfect or perfection even real? No, of course not, but their relationship was as close to perfect as it could be. To this day, my father still buys my mom flowers every Friday and tells her how much he loves her.

So there you have it. That was what I grew up seeing and believing. I believed that every man was like him and I'd meet the one who would sweep me off my feet and treat me like a queen, the way my father treated my mother. Growing up, I took pride in the fact that my parents were happy and stayed together when all my friends' parents were divorcing.

I honestly didn't think or expect men to be so fucking complicated. They're like a big rubber band, stretching out towards what they think they want, then snapping back when things start to get too comfortable. I had a talk with my mom about this very thing and she couldn't relate because she'd never experienced it. Lucky her. It was all I seemed to experience over the last, oh I don't know, ten years of dating.

I had my first boyfriend at the age of fifteen. Did he really count? After all, his brain wasn't anywhere near mature enough to comprehend relationships with girls. The only thing they focused on that young was how quickly they could get into our pants. They would do or say anything to make us swoon and eventually we'd give in and have sex. But that wasn't me. I was nowhere near ready for sex at that age.

I waited until I was sixteen when I met "the one" and his name was Kyle Stone. We'd dated for a couple of months, had sex, and then he suddenly broke it off with me when the new girl, Taylor Bradford, transferred to our school. The devastation he left behind was unbearable. My first heartbreak, and we all know first heartbreaks are the hardest. We can't even begin to comprehend what the hell happened, let alone question ourselves at what we did wrong. It took me over six months to get over Kyle and that kind of heartbreak was something I'd never forget.

After spending the next couple of years dating different guys and failing at any type of relationship, I gave up and went off to college, focusing on my passion: photography and writing. I was a natural. My father told me I was born with a camera in my hand. Silly man. I knew I wasn't, but he said I had a gift at capturing people's real emotions. People may lie about how they feel, but the camera never did. I could photograph the happiest of couples, but sometimes, their pictures told a different story. When I took countless pictures of my parents over the years, they still looked the same in every one of them, a reflection of their happiness and love. Okay, you get the point about my parents and how I was raised. My expectations were high, maybe too high and unrealistic.

While I was in college, I took on a job as an assistant to Gerard Truman, one of the greatest photographers in New York. He was edgy, cool, and had a great eye. He told me I had a promising future and he could see magazine shoots such as *Vogue, Cosmopolitan*, and even *Time*. I dated here and there in college but never would commit to any type of relationship. Ha, who was I kidding? It wasn't me who couldn't commit, it was the variety of boys—and yes, I said boys—I dated. After numerous rejections and totally feeling like a failure in the dating world, I decided to take a good look at myself. Maybe I was too needy. I didn't think I was, and I certainly didn't act like it. I was a strong, independent person, and neediness wasn't a trait of mine. But, after the countless rejections, I began to think there was something wrong with me and that I was the problem, a cycle that went on throughout my college years before I discovered I knew better.

After I graduated, I got a job at a photography studio. But, working for someone else didn't sit well with me, plus a studio setting wasn't my thing. I felt trapped and my creative abilities felt stifled, so I decided to start my own freelance photography business. I updated my portfolio and pounded the streets of New York, showing off my work with the hopes it would catch the attention of someone, anyone who would hire me. I created a website and advertised on every social media platform I could find. Slowly, business started to trickle in, and with the help of my event planner friend, Natalie, I photographed birthday parties, anniversary parties, weddings, and any other event she was hired for. Word about my work spread, a couple small magazine companies hired me, and after a year of getting my business off the ground and making decent money, I was able to move out of my parents' home and into an apartment of my own. I not only had the income from my photography business, but I also earned money monthly from my blog: "The Dating Adventures of Eloise." It was fun, sassy, and all me. Women loved to hear about my failed relationship after relationship because they could relate and somehow it didn't make them feel so alone.

I was twenty-three years old, an entrepreneur, and I lived on my own. My life was great, but I still felt like something was missing. And that something was a man/relationship. I had a lot to offer and why wouldn't I want to share that with someone special? I was independent, had my own business and my own money. After taking a brief hiatus from the dating world, I was ready to dive into it again. How bad could it be? I was older now and the men I would date had to be more mature. Shit, was I wrong.

Two years later, still treading the dating world and with no luck at finding Mr. Right, it had become apparent to me that all men were assholes and all built from the same genetically defected douchebag cloth. My photography business was on top, my blog was even bigger, but the men I dated all sucked.

My self-esteem over the years went to shit from these experiences, as did all the other women's that were part of my blog. One day, I woke up and finally realized it had nothing to do with me. The moment I decided to take a break and focus on

#*Delete*

self-love, I met a man named Luke. He was older, divorced, and had two kids. The older part didn't bother me because older guys generally had their shit together. Right? He approached me, introduced himself, and we got to talking. Besides being super cute and adorable, he had a great and fun personality. We clicked right on the spot, but there was something about him that wasn't sitting right with me. My intuition was telling me things I didn't want to hear and I was in no way listening. We had a connection and that was all I cared about.

We exchanged numbers and had some deep conversations. Then the flirting started and it was exciting. We went on a few dates when he didn't have the kids and I wasn't busy, and generally texted each other every day. Sometimes all day long. The more I got to know him, the more I found how broken he really was. My intuition was still on point, but that didn't bother me. We had a connection.

He had just started a new job he didn't feel was up to his potential, his financial situation was in the toilet, and his ex-wife was a total bitch. Did I mention he drank? It seemed to be a daily thing with him. So the fact that he might potentially be an alcoholic crept inside me. Here I was this confident, independent, and financially stable woman, dating an older man who had way too much baggage. Ask me why I didn't run as fast as I could. Again, I was blinded by the fact that we had this weird type of connection thing between us and that maybe I could save him. I saw a glimmer of hope because it was what I did. I attracted the type of men who needed to be saved.

Then one day, out of the clear blue, the text messages became scarce. He wasn't texting as much as he did and I felt like I was doing all the talking when we did text. Because my intuition was still kicking me in the ass, I decided to call him one day to find out what was going on. It was then he told me he felt we were getting too close and he needed to figure out his life and focus solely on that and his kids. Needless to say, I was blindsided by that one. I had fallen for a man who had made mistake after mistake in life, was seemingly depressed, and drank himself to sleep every night. He told me that he wasn't in any position to date at that moment. Then why the hell did he pursue me the way he did? He even went so far as to say that maybe he shouldn't have asked me out the few times we saw each other. Who the hell says that after the fact?

The real kicker was the day before our enlightened conversation, he told me how much he really liked me and even called me his angel. I couldn't understand for the life of me why I could have my life figured out at the age of twenty-five, yet I couldn't figure out a man and why he behaved the way he did. After pulling back for a couple of weeks, he wormed his way back into my life and I let him. Mistake number two. The flirting became heavy once again and then he did the unthinkable act: the plunge and lunge. He kissed me, not once, but twice, then disappeared.

#Delete

Chapter Two

Eloise

I was lying in bed looking through our text messages, trying to figure out where things went wrong. I couldn't find anything, but I needed to try and move on. But what was I moving on from? A broken alcoholic man who didn't have his life together? He was every kind of wrong, and I knew it from the first time I met him, but I didn't want to see it because I was lonely and he walked into my life when I was most vulnerable. That was what I did. I over analyzed these situations and spent too much time thinking about them. But now, I was taking my power back. I would no longer fall victim to these idiots we called men and let them have control over my emotional state. I did something I hadn't done before. I deleted his number.

I had never deleted a guy's number. My contact list was filled with guys I'd dated over the years. I suppose I kept them because somewhere in the back of my mind, I had this little bit of hope they'd call or send a text and then I would know who it was, even if it was a couple of years later. I held on to this notion that maybe they would miss me. Stupidity on my part, I know. I was fully aware of how pathetic I sounded. But now, things were going to change. With one swipe, I went through my phone and deleted the number of every guy I had dated. It felt good and empowering.

"I'm so proud of you," my friend Natalie spoke.

"Me too." Claire smiled.

"Thanks." I took a sip of my coffee. "Things are going to be different now. "By the way, where's Scarlett? I thought she was meeting us here."

"She was going to, but Hannah woke up with a fever this morning and Jeff had to go out of town on a business trip," Natalie spoke.

"With your new empowerment, I'm assuming you're over Luke now?" Claire asked.

I sighed as I set down my coffee cup.

"I still have some unfinished business with him. The thing I don't understand is why he pursued me in the first place, knowing full well his life was shit and he didn't want to date anyone."

"Maybe he just wanted sex," Claire spoke. "That's all most guys want anyway. They aren't looking for anything long term anymore. They want their cake and eat it too." She smiled.

"Don't even question it. He's not worth it. Plus, did you really want to play step-mommy to his monster children?" Natalie asked. "You're only twenty-five. Far too young to take on any sort of kid responsibility. Not to mention his excessive drinking habit."

"I know and I thought of that." I looked down at my coffee cup as I traced the rim with my finger. "I mean, I know he wasn't good for me and he'd eventually drag me down the same drain his life was stuck in, but he was fun, and I liked our conversations and our time together."

"You haven't even slept with him," Claire spoke as she

reached across the table and placed her hand on my arm. "Not to mention he did the plunge and lunge."

"Thank God we didn't sleep together. But it's not like he didn't want to," I spoke.

"Here's what I think," Natalie chimed in. "I think it's the whole rejection part of it. He was the straw that broke the camel's back for you because you expected more from him since he was older. We all know you don't handle rejection very well." She smirked.

"All that's changing now." I smiled. "My problem is I always get too emotionally attached right out of the gate and I'm not doing that anymore. I flipped the switch and turned off all my emotions."

"*You* can't do that," Claire spoke.

"I can and I have." I smiled. "Plus, I know my self-worth and I have standards."

Both girls rolled their eyes at the same time.

"So now what? Are you just going to swear off men?" Natalie asked.

"No." I smirked. "I'm going to get inside the minds of them."

"Really?" Natalie sighed. "And how are you going to do that?"

"By going out with a bunch of different guys and interviewing them." I took a sip of my coffee.

"You can't be serious!" Claire laughed.

"I am. You'll see. I have a plan." I arched my brow. "By the way, Claire, how's the new job working out?"

"Great. I love my boss. He's so nice and I'm really liking it there. Kenny just met him the other day and told me that I needed to quit."

"Why?" I asked.

"Because he's young, super-hot, and rich." She smirked.

I rolled my eyes.

"I would never be interested in him anyway, he's a serial dater. Every night, he has a new woman he goes out with. I think he has a relationship phobia."

"See!" I pointed at her. "If guys can do it, so can I!" I smiled as I held up my coffee cup.

I met Claire, Natalie, and Scarlett my freshman year of college. We formed a little posse and have been inseparable ever since. Natalie is an event planner, Claire is a graphic designer, and Scarlett is a stay-at-home mom. She and Jeff were high school sweethearts. He was another rare find, like my dad. He was a good guy, and when she got pregnant a year and a half ago, he asked her to marry him and now they're a happy little family. He works on Wall Street and has a fantastic job, one that allows Scarlett to stay home with Hannah. I wasn't sure how long her stay-at-home mommy status was going to last, though. I could tell she was starting to lose herself. We all tried to convince her to get a part time job, but Jeff wouldn't hear of it. He wanted her home raising their daughter. I could potentially see some trouble in their future if she didn't stand up for herself.

****

#Delete

After my photo shoot, I grabbed some dinner and headed home. Sitting on the couch with my knees up, I stabbed a piece of sweet and sour chicken from the carton and brought it to my mouth. The *Gilmore Girls* played in the background, but I wasn't paying attention. My mind was too busy thinking about the plan I was putting together for my blog. I finished my sweet and sour chicken, set the container on the coffee table, grabbed my laptop, and signed into my Match account, weeding through the seventy-five messages I received in the last two days. I picked the seven that I thought were the best and set up a date for every night of the week with a different guy. Now I know you might think this was nothing but pure desperation on my part, but I can assure you it wasn't. I was no longer looking for a relationship or the perfect man. I had a plan to put into action for my blog. The women who followed it depended on me to give them answers and guidance. But first, I needed to give Luke a piece of my mind and put closure on him.

I pulled up my text messages. *Shit*. I forgot I had deleted his number. My mind pondered. I knew the area code and the first two numbers and the last four. It was that third number that I couldn't quite think of. Ah, I remembered it and my fingers went to work.

"You're an asshole. Plain and simple. I can't believe I wasted my time with someone like you. You are a pathetic alcoholic who will never amount to anything. So keep trying to figure your life out and good luck. Someone like you will always be destined to stay at the bottom. Peace out, motherfucker! BTW, don't ever text me again!"

I let out a deep breath as I hit the send button. With a smile on my face, I signed into my blog and changed the name from *The Dating Adventures of Eloise* to *The Chronicles of #Delete*. My fingers typed away at the victory that was mine. He was gone, done, and a memory that was now forgotten. As I finished, my phone dinged with a text message. Looking over, I narrowed my eye at his number. I didn't care what he had to say, but I had to check anyway and then delete it. When I opened the text message, I looked at it in confusion.

"Hello. Your text message had me in tears with laughter. You're quite a little spitfire and I'm assuming your boyfriend broke up with you or something. If this text was meant for him, I'm sorry to say that he didn't get it. Apparently, you sent this by mistake to the wrong number. Thank you though. This totally made my day."

What the fuck? I stared at the number I sent the text message to very carefully. *Shit. Shit. Shit.* I was ninety percent sure I had the right number. Apparently, I didn't, so I sent an apology text.

"I'm so sorry for that text. I had already deleted the guy's number and thought I had it correct. I was going off memory, which obviously proved not to be a good idea. Anyway, I apologize for the mix up, but I'm happy I made your day." I attached the smiley face emoji and hit send.

Chapter Three

Christian

My phone dinged with a text message, and when I looked at it, I noticed it was from that same number as just a few moments ago. I lightly shook my head as I read it and a small smile crossed my lips.

"Someone sexting you?" Peter smirked as he walked into my office.

"Nah. I got this bizarre text message a few minutes ago. Here, read this." I handed him my phone.

"And you're sure this isn't from one of the million women you date?" He laughed.

"I've never seen that number before in my life. So yes, I'm sure. Besides, I'm not an alcoholic, I have my life figured out, and I'm at the top, not the bottom." I smiled.

"True. But you are an asshole and sometimes a motherfucker. So, she's got that right." He handed my phone back to me.

"Very funny. Are you and Jimmy doing anything tonight?"

"I'm not. Why?"

"I thought the three of us could head over to Hellcat Annie's for some beer and food while we discuss an account."

"You're actually free of a woman tonight?" His brow raised.

"No one worth asking out at the moment. Plus, we need to go over the Fire Line account and what better way to do it than having a bro's night at Hellcat Annie's?" I smirked.

"Sounds good to me. I'll go tell Jimmy to cancel any plans he has."

"I'll meet you guys there around eight o'clock. I'm going to go home and change first."

When I got home, I jumped into the shower and quickly changed into something more casual. Picking up my phone, I decided to respond back to the last message she sent.

"I found it quite entertaining. I must apologize for our species and the fact that he must have done something really shitty to warrant that text. Smart move deleting his number. He's not worth it. Move on."

As I finished buttoning the last button on my shirt, my phone dinged with a text message.

"Thank you. No need to apologize for your species. You can't help that you all come from the same whirlpool of douchebag central. I know he's not worth it and I have moved on. All is good now."

Same whirlpool of douchebag central? I let out a chuckle.

"We're not all douchebags. There are some decent guys in the world."

"Really? Are you a decent guy?"

"I like to think so, at least most of the time. I will admit I do have douchebag tendencies here and there, but that all depends on how crazy the girl is."

"So it's the woman's fault that guys are douchebags?"

I took a seat on the edge of the bed.

"Sometimes. If they're whiny, needy, and unbearable, then yes. It's times like that when we need to be douchebags."

"Did you ever stop to think that women act like that because of the douchebaggery of men?"

I laughed.

"Is 'douchebaggery' even a word?" I asked.

"Lol. I don't know."

"Thank you for the stimulating conversation, but I need to leave now. I'm meeting some friends for drinks," I replied.

"Have a good night and do me a favor and don't be a douchebag tonight."

"I'll try not to be. Have a good night as well."

I got up from the bed, shaking my head and smiling. This girl was kind of funny. I grabbed my wallet and key and hailed a cab to Hellcat Annie's.

Chapter Four

Eloise

"What are you doing?" Natalie asked as I answered the phone.

"Watching *Gilmore Girls*."

"Get changed and meet me and Scarlett at Hellcat Annie's."

"I thought Scarlett couldn't go out because Hannah was sick?"

"Jeff's flight got cancelled and he couldn't catch another flight out today, so he's home and told her he'd take care of Hannah if she wanted to go out."

"When are you meeting?" I asked.

"We're on our way now. Claire has a family dinner at her parents' house, so she can't join us."

"Okay. I'll get changed and head over there."

"Great. See you soon."

I really didn't feel like going out, but I knew if I didn't, I'd never hear the end of it. I got up from the couch, turned the TV off, and changed my clothes for a night of drinks and laughter with my girls.

When I walked through the door of Hellcat Annie's, I spotted Scarlett and Natalie sitting at a table. Natalie waved me over when she saw me.

"Hello." I smiled as I kissed Scarlett's cheek and then Natalie's. "Oh, is this for me?" I asked as I looked down at the cosmopolitan on the table.

"Yes. I took the liberty of ordering it for you." Natalie smiled.

"Thanks."

I sat down in my chair and picked up my glass.

"How's Hannah doing?" I asked Scarlett.

"The doctor said she's teething. She's been a nightmare lately. She was screaming her head off when I walked out the door. Poor Jeff." She smirked.

"You don't really mean that," both Natalie and I spoke at the same time.

"No, I don't." She laughed.

"So," I slightly leaned across the table, "tomorrow will be the official day I'm kicking off T*he Chronicles of #Delete* on my blog."

"What?" Scarlett asked in confusion.

"You're going to love this." Natalie grinned as she took a sip of her drink.

"#Delete is the new project for my blog. After I go on multiple dates and interview the guys, I will #Delete their ass from my phone."

"Why?" she asked.

"So she's not tempted to text any of them when they don't text her," Natalie spoke as she rolled her eyes.

"That is not true." I cocked my head. "I'm changing my game in the dating world. I have given up trying to find the perfect guy who doesn't behave like a douchebag. I'll collect the information and then pass it along to my ladies, via my blog." I smiled. "In fact, I already have dates set up for the next seven nights."

"All from Match, I presume?" Scarlett spoke.

"As a matter of fact, yes."

"But why?" She gave me a weird look.

"Why not? My goal is to help empower women when it comes to dating a guy who starts behaving badly. I'm not doing this with the hopes of getting into a relationship with someone. Those days, at least for now, are over until I can get inside the head of a man and truly know what's going on in his feeble little mind."

"Wait a minute." Scarlett shook her head. "Isn't Match.com a place where guys and girls actually want to meet someone with the possibility of having a relationship? Isn't that why they join in the first place?"

"Yes. And?" I arched my brow.

I took the last sip of my drink and held my finger up to signal our waitress over to our table.

"I'm headed over to the bar." A gorgeous man smiled as he stopped by our table. "What can I get you?" he asked as he looked down at my empty glass.

I stared at him from head to toe. Six foot one, maybe two. Sandy brown hair that was perfectly styled. The bluest eyes that could be noticed from far across the room. Eyes that reminded me of beautiful tropical waters. His smile was panty-melting as was the light stubble he sported along his masculine jawline. I gulped.

"A cosmopolitan." I graciously smiled as I swallowed the lump in my throat.

"One cosmopolitan coming right up." He winked. "Ladies, do you need a refill?" he asked Natalie and Scarlett.

"No. We're good," Natalie responded.

The moment he walked away, I let out the breath I'd held inside me.

"Oh my God." My mouth dropped as I looked at them.

"He's a hottie." Scarlett smiled.

"He's a player," Natalie spoke. "A guy who you'd fall for in a second, full emotions and all. I see the look on your face, Eloise. It's already happening! Stop right there!" She pointed at me. #Delete, remember?"

"You're right." I put up my hand. "He is a player. I've got that whole player vibe running through me."

"Here you are." The gorgeous man smiled as he set my drink down in front of me.

"Thank you." I felt the heat rise in my cheeks. "How much do I owe you?"

"Your drink is on me. The only thing I ask in return is your name." He smirked.

I swallowed hard.

"Eloise."

With a smile, he cocked his head.

"What a beautiful name. I'm Christian." He held out his hand.

I looked at it for a moment with fear coursing through my veins. Slowly lifting my hand, I placed mine in his and lightly shook it while my knees trembled underneath the table.

"It was nice to meet you, Eloise."

"You too, Christian. Thanks again for the drink."

"The pleasure was all mine." He gave me a wink and walked back to his table.

I sat there, staring at him while he walked away as Natalie and Scarlett waved their hands in front of my face.

"Shit," Natalie spoke. "Eloise, focus!"

I snapped back into reality and inhaled a sharp breath.

"You aren't that woman anymore, remember?" Scarlett spoke. "You're on a mission and he's not part of it. Don't let the girls who read your blog down."

"You're right."

We talked for a while longer, finished our drinks, and headed home. As I left the restaurant and was trying to hail a cab, I heard someone call my name.

"Eloise?"

I turned, only to see Christian approaching me.

"Hi." I smiled.

"Hi. Is there a chance I can get your phone number?"

The butterflies in my stomach woke up and filled me with a fluttering sensation that wouldn't stop. *Shit. Shit. Shit.* I wanted to give it to him. It was on the tip of my tongue. My heart was screaming YES, but my head screamed NO, and then I thought about my mission.

"I'm flattered you want it, but I can't give it to you. I'm sorry."

"You can't or you won't?" He smirked.

"I won't. I just got out of a relationship and I have things I need to figure out."

"Okay, but who said anything about a relationship? I thought maybe we could talk and meet for dinner some time."

"I didn't say I wanted a relationship with you." I cocked my head. "I'm simply letting you know that I'm not interested in going out with anyone right now."

His eye narrowed at me as he slowly nodded his head. Fuck, he was so sexy and this broke my rapidly beating heart, for I knew his type, and it was his type that would send me spiraling down into the depths of emotional hell.

"I understand. Have a good night, Eloise." He held up his hand and hailed a cab for me.

"Thank you, Christian. Same to you."

I climbed into the back of the cab and Christian shut the door.

"Where to, lady?" the cab driver asked.

"360 West 43rd Street, please," I spoke as the cab pulled away and I lifted my hand, giving Christian a small wave goodbye.

Chapter Five

Christian

"So, did you get her number?" Jimmy asked as we sat at the round table in my office.

"Nah. She wouldn't give it to me."

Peter nearly spit out his coffee.

"What? Someone actually turned down the great Christian Blake?" He laughed.

"She said something about just getting out of a relationship and she wasn't looking to date anyone right now." I sighed.

"Oh well, on to the next." Jimmy smiled.

I couldn't stop thinking about her all night. The moment my eyes saw her sitting at the table with her friends, something struck inside me. I felt this overwhelming need to want to get to know her. She was gorgeous. Five foot seven with long brown wavy hair that perfectly flowed over her shoulders. Her green eyes sparkled like shiny emeralds that could light up even the darkest of rooms. Eyes that could hold the universe within them. I sat at my table and watched the way her perfectly shaped lips gave way to a smile. A smile that illuminated her beautiful face.

We shared a moment, and even though that moment was brief, it would be one I'd remember for a long time.

"Bro, are you okay?" Peter asked.

"What?" I blankly stared at him.

"You zoned out for a moment," Jimmy spoke. "You still thinking about that girl?"

"No way." I got up from my chair. "I don't do shit like that and you know it." I looked at my watch. "It's time for our weekly productivity meeting. I'll meet you in the conference room."

Walking over to my desk, I picked up my phone and held it in my hand. Opening my messages, I decided to send a text message to the girl.

"Just checking in to see how last night was and to let you know that I wasn't a douchebag."

As I was walking to my meeting, a reply came through.

"Lol. I'm happy to hear you refrained from being a douchebag. My night was exciting! Well, maybe not too exciting. Just had a girls' night with my friends."

I sent her a message back as I walked into the conference room.

"Girls' night is good. At least you weren't home moping around over that jerk. I'm off to a meeting now. Catch ya later!"

"I don't mope. I'm better than that. Have a good meeting and I'll catch ya later."

I let out a light chuckle before taking my seat and starting the meeting.

****

When I got home, I quickly showered and changed for my date with a woman named Cheyenne. I'd met her last week at an art gallery opening. She was attractive and newly divorced. She told me she'd only been married a couple of years and it was the biggest mistake of her life. One she wouldn't make again. Her vibe told me that she was looking to have some fun and that was all I wanted too. So, I called her last night after I got home and set up the date. Was she Eloise? Absolutely not, but I couldn't let her rejection of me interfere with dating other women. I'd been in a couple of relationships in my life and they just never seemed right. I wasn't against relationships. They just weren't for me. At least at this point in my life. Maybe in ten years, I'd feel differently. I just dated different women all the time without the hassles of being in a relationship. Life was too short to commit to one person. Especially at my age of thirty. I was in my prime years, building my advertising firm, making a shitload of money, and enjoying everything life had to offer, including beautiful women.

"Sorry I'm late," I spoke as I leaned over and kissed Cheyenne's cheek. "Traffic was horrible tonight and I was almost killed twice when the cabbie decided to cut a few people off."

"No problem." She smiled.

I took the seat across from her and looked over the wine list.

"Is there a certain type of wine you prefer?" I asked.

"I would actually prefer a bottle of champagne," she replied.

Wow. That caught me off guard. First date and she's already expecting the best.

"Okay. Champagne, it is."

The waitress brought our bottle of Champagne and then proceeded to take our dinner order. Of course, Cheyenne ordered the most expensive thing on the menu. I could already tell she was high maintenance, especially with the amount of Botox she had injected into her skin at such a young age. The more we talked, or should I say, she talked, the more bored I became. When she excused herself to the bathroom, I pulled my phone from my pocket. Pulling up my messages, I sent a text to that girl.

"Hi. I'm on a date and terribly bored."

"You're not the only one. I'm also on a date and my face is about ready to hit the plate."

I let out a light laugh.

"He can't be worse than mine. She's a buyer. As in handbags and shoes, for herself."

"Lol. My guy is a financial advisor, and for the last two hours, all he's talked about is Roth IRAs and shit. Did I mention he's wearing a bow tie?"

"You poor girl."

"He's coming back from the bathroom. We'll talk later?"

"Of course. Cut the date short if he's that bad. If you need my help, let me know."

"Thanks. But, like the lady I am, I'll finish it out and then let him down gently."

#Delete

"Good girl."

Cheyenne walked back to the table and sat down in her seat.

"Who were you texting?" she asked.

I gave her an odd look because, frankly, that was none of her business.

"One of my colleagues. There's a work issue," I replied.

"Do you always do work when you're on a date? My ex used to do that all the time and it was so annoying."

I wanted to tell her that he probably wasn't working and more than likely texting other women he was seeing on the side. Once we finished dinner, I paid the bill and we stepped out into the brightly lit New York City streets. Cheyenne ran her finger down my chest as I was trying to say good bye.

"How about we go to my place for a nightcap or two?" She smiled.

"As nice as that sounds, I'm afraid I can't. I have a very early meeting tomorrow."

"Poo poo." She pouted.

I sighed, as I couldn't wait to get away from her.

"Thanks for dinner. I had a great time, Christian. Call me?" Her brow arched.

"I had a nice time too," I lied. "I'll call you," I lied again.

I leaned over and lightly kissed her cheek before putting her in a cab and sending her home.

Stepping into my bedroom, I stripped out of my clothes and

put on a pair of black pajama bottoms. Picking up my phone, I sent that girl a text.

"Has your date ended?"

"Yes. I'm home safe and sound. But the talk of Roth IRAs won't stop circling around in my head. How about you?"

"Yes. I'm home. She wanted to go back to her place. I politely declined."

"I'm shocked. You turned down sex with a woman? What kind of man are you?"

"A man who looks at a woman for more than just sex. I don't sleep with every woman I take out. By the way, is there a chance I can get your name? After all, we seem to be texting quite a bit."

"Wouldn't that ruin the mystery of us?" she replied. *"I kind of like not knowing who you are."*

"I suppose you're right. Two strangers talking by one accidental text is different. But I still need to call you something other than 'that girl.'"

"How about Digits?" she replied. *"Since I sent you my digits by accident."*

"Digits. I like it. You are now officially in my phone as Digits."

"Great. I'll think of a name for you. Enjoy the rest of your evening. I need to go to bed now and sleep off the massive numbers running through my head from all that financial advice I received."

"Lol. Good night, Digits."

#Delete

"Good night, Mobile Man. Oh, there's your name."

"I like it." I smiled as I replied.

"Me too."

Chapter Six

Eloise

I was in the middle of shooting a couple's engagement pictures in Central Park when my phone dinged. As we were on our way to our next location, I pulled my phone from pocket and checked my text messages.

"Hi! I was just thinking about you. How are you doing? I'm surprised I haven't heard from you."

I glared at the number and realized it was from Luke. He was surprised he hadn't heard from me? Was he serious? My fingers went to typing town.

"Why are you thinking about me? By the way, I'm doing fantastic! I would ask how you're doing, but I don't really care, which is the reason why you haven't heard from me."

A few moments later, he replied.

"Wow. Just wow! Where the hell did that come from?"

"#Delete," I quickly responded and then deleted his number.

"What does that mean?!" His number popped up again.

I ignored him, swiped to the left and deleted his number because I couldn't spend any more time or energy on his dumb

#Delete

ass. I finished the photo shoot and headed to Starbucks for a coffee and to start writing my blog post about my date last night. I had a couple of hours to spare before I had to get home and change for another date.

As I was typing away and sipping my coffee, I heard a loud voice enter through the door.

"Hey, you!" Claire smiled as she walked over and hugged me. "What are you doing here?"

"I just finished a photo shoot and I'm blogging." I smiled. "Aren't you supposed to be at work?"

"I'm on a coffee run for the guys." She rolled her eyes. "Hey." She sat down in the chair across from me. "My boss is having a party this Saturday at his place and invited me. Kenny is going on that camping weekend with the guys and said I wasn't allowed to go unless you, Nat, or Scarlett went with me."

"Is he really that worried about your boss?" I cocked my head.

"He has insecurities. You know that. Remember, his last girlfriend left him for another guy."

"I get that, but he needs to get over it! Why are you with him if he doesn't trust you?"

"He trusts me. It's the other men he doesn't trust. Say you'll go. Please. Pretty, pretty please."

"I have a date Saturday night, remember?" I arched my brow.

"BFFs before dates. You know the rule, Eloise. Think of the guys you'll meet at the party. You can blog about them!" She smirked.

"That defeats the purpose of #Delete."

"Maybe not. Get their number, go out on a date, interview them, and then #Delete their ass!"

As she was trying to convince me to cancel my date for Saturday night, my phone dinged with a text message from Mobile Man. The corners of my lips curved into a small smile.

"Top of the day to you. Hope it's a good one. And I hope the numbers have stopped in your head."

"Who texted you?" Claire asked. "Why are you smiling?"

I hadn't told any of them yet about Mobile Man because I didn't think we'd be talking as much as we were. I guess it was time to let the cat out of the bag.

"I'm talking to Mobile Man." I casually smiled as I sipped my coffee.

"Who?" Her brows furrowed.

"Last week, when I was telling off Luke via text, I accidentally sent it to the wrong phone number. This guy responded and we just started texting each other, like every day."

"Who is this guy?"

"I don't know. I call him 'Mobile Man' and he calls me 'Digits.'"

"Okay, that's fucking weird. What's his name?"

"I don't know and I don't want to know. The mystery of it is exciting!" I smirked.

"So you're texting some random guy every day and you don't know anything about him?"

"You are correct." I lightly nodded.

"You, my friend, have gone completely insane. He could be married for all you know."

"He's not. He was on a date last night just like I was. We were both bored so we started texting each other."

I picked up my phone and replied to him.

"Hi! Top of the day to you too! The numbers have stopped, thank god! How's your day going?"

"Put that phone down and tell me more!" she demanded.

"There's nothing more to tell. I know not one thing about him except that he doesn't sleep with every woman he takes out."

"Yeah, right." She rolled her eyes and then looked at her watch. "Shit. I need to order the coffees and go. So, yes to Saturday?" She stood up and placed her hand on her hip.

"Fine. I'll go."

"Yay! It'll be fun. Just you wait and see!"

As soon as she walked away, my phone dinged again.

"The day is good. A lot of contracts are being signed today and money is being made. Couldn't ask for anything more."

"So you're in corporate business? Just a simple yes or no, please."

I didn't want to know anything about him. This game was fun and it allowed me to be anyone I wanted and anyone he wanted.

"Yes. I'm in corporate business. What do you do?"

I needed to think quick.

"I'm in the social media relations business."

"Ah, I see. Care to elaborate on that?"

"I like to write."

"Are you like a journalist or something?"

"Something like that."

"Listen, Digits, I have to head into a meeting. Catch ya later?"

"Okay. Catch ya later."

****

I slipped into my tight-fitted, spaghetti-strap black dress and shoved my feet into a pair of black Kate Spade heels with a peep toe and a bow. Tonight's date was with a man named Aaron. According to his profile, he was thirty years old and a high school science teacher. As I was walking out the door, a text message came through from a number I didn't recognize.

"Hi, Eloise. I really enjoyed our night together last night. How about we set up another date?"

Shit. It was from Frankie, the financial guy. Because he was too busy trying to feed my soul full of financial advice, I didn't get to ask him many questions when it came to women. The only thing I could get out of him was that he liked to wait a couple of days after a date to text the girl back. So why the hell was he texting me already?

"Hi, Frankie. You're a nice guy, but I don't think another date is such a good idea. I really wasn't feeling a connection. I'm sorry."

"No problem. I wasn't feeling it either, but I thought I would give you a second chance," he replied.

Rolling my eyes, I swiped to the left and deleted his boring ass.

When I reached PRINT, a restaurant over in Hell's Kitchen, I walked inside and looked around.

"Can I help you?" the young redheaded hostess asked.

"I'm meeting someone here."

"Aaron?" she asked.

"Yes." I smiled.

"Follow me, please."

I followed her to the table where Aaron sat. He was cute, I won't lie. Clean cut, dark hair, baby face. I was sure the girls in his class swooned over him every day.

"My God." He grinned as he stood up from his chair. "You are more beautiful in person." He kissed my cheek.

"Thank you." I smiled.

"I took the liberty of ordering a bottle of white wine. I hope that's okay."

"I like white wine." The corners of my mouth slightly curved upwards as I took the seat across from him.

We talked about his job, my job, his family, and my family. We had a few things in common and he seemed easy to talk to. I was anxiously waiting for the perfect opportunity to slip my questions in. He caught me off guard when he reached across the table and took hold of my hand, interlacing our fingers.

"Can we just get married? Because I'm ninety-nine percent sure that we're soulmates and one hundred percent sure that I'm in love."

I sat there staring at him in disbelief. Suddenly, I let out a light laugh.

"That's sweet. You're funny."

"Why is that funny?" he asked in a serious tone. "I mean it. I know when I'm in love, and right now, I'm in love with you, Eloise. You're gorgeous, you have a great personality, and I know you're my soulmate. I can feel it in every fiber in my body."

Pulling my hand away from his, I spoke, "Well, Aaron, can you please tell the fibers in your body to stop feeling it." I smirked to try and lighten the moment.

"No, I won't!" he loudly voiced.

I glanced around the restaurant to make sure no one was staring at us. Slowly getting up from the table, I grabbed my purse.

"I think I'm going to call it a night." I pulled some cash out from my wallet and threw it on the table. "I can pay for my own dinner. Thanks." I scurried out of the restaurant and climbed

#Delete

into a cab that was sitting at the curb.

This date was one that went very wrong. Pulling my phone from my purse, I deleted Aaron's number and then sent a text message to Mobile Man.

"I just had to exit a date early because the guy told me that he was in love with me, he knows we're soulmates, and we should get married."

A few moments later, he replied.

"How long have you known this guy?" he asked.

"I just met him tonight. What the hell is wrong with these guys?"

"Lol. You must have made his heart stop. I will say that is unusual behavior. The guy must be desperate."

"He's not desperate, he's weird. And now I can see why he's single. Shame, though, he was really cute."

"You can't always go by looks, Digits," he replied.

"Oh please, Mobile Man. You're not going to tell me that you date not-so-attractive women. It's purely physical for you guys."

"Fine. You caught me."

"Thought so."

"But it's the same with you women as well. If you don't think a guy is hot or sexy, you won't give him the time of day."

"That is not true."

"Yes, it is and you know it."

I sighed. I knew he was right, but I didn't want to admit it to him.

"Come on, Digits. Admit it."

"I'm pleading the fifth," I replied.

"Ha. That right there is your answer."

"I'm home now and going to soak in a hot bubble-filled tub. Catch ya later, Mobile Man."

"Enjoy the rest of your evening, Digits. Catch ya later."

Chapter Seven

Christian

"Who are you texting, bro? We're trying to finish this meeting so we can go home," Peter spoke.

"Digits." I set my phone down.

"Is that the girl who sent you that weird text meant for someone else?" Jimmy asked.

"Yes." I smirked.

"You two are still texting each other?" Peter furrowed his brow.

"Yep. Every day," I replied.

"But you know nothing about her?" Jimmy cocked his head.

"Nope. Nothing."

"Dude, seriously, why are you still talking to her?" Peter asked.

"Because I like to. She's fun and a lot easier to talk to than half the women I date."

"I bet she's ugly as fuck." Jimmy laughed.

Peter let out a laugh and pointed at him.

"So what? It's not like I'm dating her. We're just texting."

"And you're going to sit there and tell me that you're not the least bit curious as to what she looks like?" Peter raised his brow.

"Nope. Not at all. She's just someone I like to talk to via text."

"Yeah. Okay, bro." Jimmy laughed.

We ended our late night meeting and I headed home. The truth was I would love to know what Digits looked like. I was curious because she seemed to have such a great personality. But, unfortunately, I would never know because she liked keeping herself a secret. Nonetheless, she was a delightful distraction from the humdrum of the daily grind.

****

Eloise

After my relaxing bath, I climbed into bed with my laptop and began editing some of the engagement photos I took, for I promised the happy couple that I would have them ready by Monday. As I edited the pictures and stared at the images that so profoundly captured their happiness, my mind began to wander about the last two dates I'd had. Financial guy didn't work out because I couldn't get a word in edgewise beneath all the financial advice he spewed. Soulmate guy didn't work because he wouldn't shut the fuck up about how in love with me he was and the thought that we should get married. Maybe Match wasn't a good way to do my research. I sent a text message to the rest of the five guys, unapologetically canceled

#Delete

our dates, and then proceeded to #Delete their asses from my phone.

****

Natalie sat on the edge of my bed as I sat on the floor in front of my full-length mirror and applied my makeup.

"I'm proud of you for cancelling those dates. I didn't think you could go through with it," she spoke.

"It's not that I couldn't go through with it." I looked at her after meticulously applying my eyeliner. "They weren't the right guys to interview."

"Then who are the right guys to interview?" She narrowed her eye at me.

"The ones I'm going to randomly meet at bars, clubs, coffee shops, etc."

She let out a light laugh. "What are you going to do? Walk up to them with your notebook and pen and ask them why they're such douchebags?"

"Pretty much." I grinned.

"Jesus, Eloise. Your issues go beyond anything I imagined."

"Actually, I only have one issue and that is trying to get inside the head of a man."

"Good luck with that. And when are you going to do this? You're booked back to back with photo shoots for the next two weeks."

"I can carve out some time. After all, I did have five more dates set up." I winked.

She got up from the bed and grabbed her purse.

"Well, keep me posted and have fun tonight with Claire. Try to keep your interviews to a minimum. You wouldn't want to embarrass her and have her co-workers thinking you're a few stacks short of mental stability."

"Thanks." I scrunched up my nose at her.

As she began to walk out of the room, she stopped and turned around.

"Speaking of a few stacks short of mental stability, who the fuck is Mobile Man? And why haven't you told me about him?"

I sighed as I rolled my eyes.

"She told you?"

"Of course she did. But the problem is that YOU didn't tell me."

"It's no big deal. He's just a guy I've been talking to. Two strangers texting each other. That's it."

"It's weird, Eloise. You don't know his name or anything about him, yet you talk to him. He could be some murderer or kidnapper for all you know."

"He's not." I rolled my eyes. "He's a nice guy. He's in business and he's always attending meetings."

"What did you tell him you do?" she asked suspiciously.

"I told him I was in the social media relations business."

"Like I said, a few stacks short of mental stability," she sighed.

#Delete

"Get out of here so I can finish getting ready." I threw one of my pillows at her.

She gave me a sly smile as she left the bedroom.

****

The cab pulled up to the tall building on East 89th Street and Claire and I climbed out.

"Nice building," I spoke as I looked up at it.

My phone dinged with a text message and when I took it from my purse, I noticed it was from Mobile Man.

"Hi there. I realized we didn't touch base today. Everything good?"

The doorman opened the door for us and Claire told him we were here for the Christian Blake party. He politely smiled and told us to take the elevator up to the 29th floor and he was in apartment B.

"Is it weird that I'm really nervous?" Claire asked as we stepped off the elevator.

"Yes. Why would you be nervous? He's your boss."

"Exactly!" She lightly hit my arm. "He's my boss! I've never seen him outside of the office."

"Calm down. He's just a person like you and me," I spoke as I knocked on apartment B and replied back to Mobile Man.

"Hi! Everything's great. Out with my girlfriend right now. You?"

"Good to hear. It's been quite a busy day. Having some

people over. Catch ya later?"

"Catch ya later!"

Some guy, a really cute guy, dressed in all black with blonde wavy hair answered the door.

"Hey, Claire." He smiled as he kissed her cheek. "Come on in."

"Hey, Peter. This is my girlfriend, Eloise."

We both looked at each other strangely.

"I think I know you." He pointed at me.

"I feel as if I know you too." I cocked my head but couldn't for the life of me remember where from.

"Wait a minute. You're that girl from Hellcat Annie's." He smiled.

I glared at him for a moment. *Shit*.

"Claire, who's your boss?" I asked.

"His name is Christian Blake. Why?"

I gulped.

"Hello, Claire," his voice spoke from behind.

"Christian." She turned around and he lightly kissed her cheek.

His eyes diverted their attention over to where I was standing as he looked at me from head to toe.

"Eloise." He took hold of my hand and brought it up to his lips. "It's nice to see you again."

#Delete

"Christian." I gave a light nod and smile.

My stomach started to flutter and my skin started to heat.

"You two know each other?" Claire asked in confusion.

"Eloise and I briefly met at Hellcat Annie's not too long ago. I had no idea she was a friend of yours."

"And I had no idea he was your boss," I spoke.

"Okay. Wow. This is weird. I need a drink. I'll be right back." She walked away.

"Would you have come if you had known I was Claire's boss?" He slyly smiled.

A waiter walked by with a tray of champagne glasses sitting upon it. Taking one, I smirked, "I don't know."

He chuckled as he took a sip of the drink he was holding.

"Please excuse me. A friend of mine just walked in." He placed his hand on my arm and it felt like it went numb.

I swallowed hard before bringing the tall glass of bubbly up to my lips. I couldn't believe he was Claire's boss. His smile, his charm, and overall appearance made me weak in the knees. But I needed to remember that he was a serial dater, according to Claire.

"Why didn't you tell me you met him?" She came up behind me.

"How the hell did I know he was your boss?"

"But you didn't even tell me that some guy approached you that night." She pouted.

"It was a brief encounter. He bought me a drink and asked for my number."

"And you didn't give it to him?" she asked with amazement.

"No. Because according to our dear friend, Natalie, he's the type I would fall for head over heels instantly. Plus, I got that whole player vibe feel from him."

"That is true. He does date different women all the damn time. I honestly don't know how he keeps them all straight. I'll be right back. One of my co-workers just walked in."

As Claire went off to talk to her co-worker, I walked around Christian's apartment, taking in at how lovely it was. What caught my attention were the white oak floors with the subtle tinted beige walls that made the living space look larger than it really was. His furniture was colored in blacks and beiges, giving off the modern urban décor style vibe. Walking over to the three-oversized floor-to-ceiling windows, I took in the dramatic city and river views, which were picturesque.

"Beautiful view, isn't it?" I heard Christian's voice come up behind me.

"It definitely is." I brought my champagne glass up to my lips. "So tell me, Mr. Blake, how does someone your age have his own advertising firm?"

"Well," he smiled, "my partners and I have talked about owning our own firm since we were kids."

"Your partners?" I cocked my head.

"Yes. Peter and Jimmy. We started our firm, Blake Group, three years ago."

"Please tell me if this is too personal, but if you're all partners, why is your name the only one on the doors?"

He chuckled. "That's because I put up the majority of the money for the company after my grandfather died."

"Ah. I see." I lightly smiled. "From what I can tell, your company seems to be doing very well for only opening its doors three years ago."

"Our company is doing extremely well. We've worked very hard and put in a lot of blood, sweat, and tears to make it happen and a success. A lot of sacrifices were made, but nothing that I've regretted. Tell me about you. What do you do?"

"I'm a freelance photographer."

"Interesting." He smirked. "What do you photograph?"

"Whatever people hire me for." I smirked back. I've done a few small magazine shoots, but mostly it's weddings, engagements, anniversary parties, and birthdays."

"I'd love to see your work someday." The corners of his mouth curved upwards.

I swallowed hard because every time he smiled, it sent my body into a blaze of fire. This was not good. Not good at all.

Chapter Eight

Eloise

I finished off my second glass of champagne and took another as the waiter walked by. Christian arched his brow at me and then looked at his watch.

"You've been here thirty minutes and that's your third glass of champagne."

"Yeah. Well. It's just so good." I winked.

"Christian, can you come over here for a moment?" a young man asked as he held his hand up.

"I'll be right back." He smiled as he lightly touched my arm.

I looked around for Claire. Damn her for leaving me like this. Pulling my phone from my purse, I sent a text message to Natalie.

"You are never going to believe whose house I'm at."

"Aren't you at that party with Claire?"

"Yes. Do you know who her boss is?" I typed with rapid fingers.

"No, should I?"

"Christian Blake!"

"How do I know that name?"

"The guy from Hellcat Annie's that bought me a drink and then asked for my phone number! The one you said to stay away from because he was a player and you could see me totally falling for him!"

"Oh shit! Omg! He's her boss?"

"YES. We've been talking. He's so fucking hot and seems really nice."

"No, Eloise! #DELETE! I don't want to see you go down that road again. Claire said herself he's a serial dater. He's the type that won't commit to anyone. You'll date a couple times, get your hopes up, he'll stop texting or calling, you'll get all pissed off and upset and then we'll have to pick you up and put you back together again. Men like Christian Blake are notorious for that."

"You're right. But he's showing interest."

"Of course he is! You're drop dead gorgeous, but I can guarantee you he only wants one thing and you know exactly what I'm talking about!"

"You're right," I replied with a sad emoji. "He's coming back my way. I'll talk to you later."

I downed the rest of my champagne and that last gulp hit me. Why didn't I eat before I came here?

He walked over to me with a panty-melting smile that sent a weakness to my knees.

"You drank that fast." He grinned.

"It's so good. I couldn't help it." I looked him up and down.

"Is something wrong?" he asked.

"No. Why?" I cocked my head.

"It's just the way you looked at me."

"You're an incredibly attractive man. I'm sure all the women look at you like that."

He stood there for a moment, his eyes burning into mine. He slowly brought his hand up and placed it on my cheek.

"And I think you are a very beautiful woman."

I could feel the heat rise throughout my face. His hand was soft as silk, and his touch froze me in place.

"Thank you," I muttered. "Could you please tell me where your bathroom is?"

"I'll show you." He smiled.

He grabbed hold of my hand and led me through the living room and down the hallway.

"Looks like someone is using it," he spoke. "You can use the one upstairs."

Still holding my hand, he led me up the stairs and to the first door on the left.

"Thank you." My lips gave way to a small smile as I went into the bathroom and shut the door.

My body was tingling from head to toe. After washing my hands and looking at myself in the mirror, I took in a deep breath and opened the door, only to find Christian standing there waiting for me. Our eyes locked on each other's and suddenly, his lips were pressed into mine. Soft, subtle, invigorating. I returned his kiss and then he looked at me. He leaned in for another and I willingly let him. His tongue met mine as our lips moved in sync. The hand that was softly placed on my cheek moved to the nape of my neck, intensifying the lip lock we were in. He slowly began pushing me back into the bathroom. *Shit*. We were going to have sex, and at this point, I didn't care. The alcohol fucked with all my senses of what was right and what was wrong. This was definitely a wrong, but I was too deep into the feeling of his hands all over my body to care. He kicked the door shut with his foot and reached his hand back and locked it.

His fingers hooked around the thin straps to the dress I was wearing, and with ease, pushed them off my shoulders, letting my dress fall to the ground. My hands fumbled with the buttons on his shirt as the heated moment made my heart race with anticipation of seeing his naked body. With one hand, he unclasped my strapless bra with ease and tossed it to the side. His hands groped my breasts as our lips stayed locked together. Soft moans escaped both of us at the same time as his hand traveled down my torso and into my panties. The light sweep of his fingers across my wet zone made me gasp.

I fumbled with his belt as he slipped off my panties. Breaking our kiss, he took a step back and stared at me while he unbuttoned his pants and slid them off his hips. Holy shit, his body rocked in all the right places. Toned, muscular, perfect. His cock, long, big, but not too big, stood tall and proud in front of me. My heart raced at the speed of light as he removed his wallet from his pants and took out a condom. After rolling it on, his hands clasped my hips and he lifted me up on the counter. Our lips met again with pleasure and my hands roamed over his body. In one thrust, he was inside me, my pussy taking him in inch by inch. I threw my head back at the pleasure as his lips explored my neck. My legs wrapped tightly around him as he deepened himself inside me. His hips moved back and forth, while his cock hit every pleasure station. The buildup was coming and I found myself standing at the edge of a cliff waiting for the moment to take the leap into euphoria. I quietly moaned so no one would hear as did he while he thrust in and out of me. My orgasm erupted and his mouth smashed into mine to quiet the feral sounds that escaped me. Tightening my legs, my body released itself to him, giving up all the pleasure I had stored up inside me. He slowed down as groans erupted in his chest and he halted as he came, pushing deep inside as my nails dug into back.

He pulled out of me and disposed of the condom in the wastebasket. Hopping off the counter, I almost fell due to the intense shaking of my legs.

"Are you okay?" Christian asked as he lightly grabbed hold of my arm.

"I'm fine. Just a leg cramp." I lightly smiled.

After putting on our clothes, he turned to me and placed his hand on my cheek.

"I want to see you again." His thumb softly stroked my skin.

I needed to play it cool in front of him and it took every bit of post sex strength I had to remain composed.

"I'm thinking this is a one-time thing. We'd been drinking and it just happened. So, I think it's best that we don't see each other again."

"You're not serious," he spoke.

#*Delete*

"Oh, I am, Mr. Blake. Now if you'll excuse me, I need to leave. I'm sure Claire is looking for me."

"Can I at least get your phone number?" he asked as I opened the bathroom door.

"No. I'm sorry. Like I said before, I'm not ready to date anyone right now."

I walked out of the bathroom, practically hyperventilating, and scurried to the front door. Taking the elevator down to the lobby, I ran out as fast as I could. Once the fresh crisp air hit my lungs, I leaned against the brick wall and placed my hands on my head. I had never done what I just did. I'd never slept with a man I didn't know and I'd never had a one-night stand. All kinds of feelings and emotions were coursing through my body. For fuck sake, why did he have to be so sexy and superb at sex? Sex was what he was after and I willingly gave in to him. How stupid could I be? Shaking my head, I pulled my phone from my purse and sent a text message to Claire.

"Hey, I'm not feeling well, so I'm going to go home."

"What's wrong?"

"I feel nausea and I have a headache. It hit me out of nowhere. Talk tomorrow?"

"Of course. Feel better. If you need anything, call me."

I walked down the street and hailed a cab home. I felt this overwhelming need to text Mobile Man.

"Hi. I'm having a bad night."

"You and me both. You okay?"

"Yeah. I'm fine. Just one of those nights where everything

seems to go wrong."

"Funny you should say that because I feel the same way," he replied. *"I'll text you later. I'm in the middle of something. Okay?"*

"Okay. Catch ya later!"

"Catch ya later, Digits!"

As soon as the cab pulled up to my building, I handed the driver some cash and climbed out. Instead of going inside and up to my apartment, I walked around the block to Didjo's, a popular bar where I'd go and sit when I needed to think.

"Hey, Eloise." Charlie smiled as he set a napkin down in front of me. "Usual?"

"Hi, Charlie. Yes, please."

He perfectly made my cosmopolitan and set it down. Picking up the glass, I took a large sip.

"You okay?" he asked. "You seem off tonight."

"Sure. If you call having sex with a total stranger in his bathroom and then running out like a frightened child okay, then I am."

He chuckled.

"Ah. I see. The good old walk of shame."

"I'd never done the walk of shame before." I finished off my drink. "Another, please."

"Chalk it up to a life experience. Everyone has to do it at least once in their lifetime," he spoke as he made me another cosmopolitan. "No big deal."

I stared at him. He was cute. I mean, I always knew he was cute, but the sudden urge to ask him questions about women jolted through me.

"How old are you, Charlie?" I asked.

"Twenty-eight." He set my drink down in front of me.

"I'm sure you have a lot of experience with women. Right?"

"Sure. I'd say so." He smiled as he wiped down the counter.

"Would you mind if I asked you a few questions?"

"Go right ahead."

Chapter Nine

Eloise

After interviewing Charlie, and three cosmopolitans later, I stumbled home. As I approached my apartment, I heard Natalie call my name from down the hall.

"Eloise?"

"Natalie? What are you doing here?"

She held up the brown bag she was carrying.

"Claire told me you left the party because you were sick, so I thought I'd swing by and bring you some chicken soup. But, by the looks of it, I don't think you're sick at all." She walked up to me and placed her nose in front of my mouth. "You've been drinking cosmopolitans."

"So?" I walked inside and kicked off my shoes.

She set the brown bag with the soup in it down on the kitchen counter.

"Where were you?"

"Didjo's around the corner." I walked into my bedroom and she followed behind.

"Why? Why did you tell Claire that you were sick and had

to leave?"

"I didn't want to be there." I stripped out of my clothes and pulled my nightshirt from my drawer.

"Did something happen with Christian?" She took a seat on the edge of the bed and narrowed her eyes at me.

"No. Why would you think that?" I went into the bathroom to wash my face.

"You scrunched up your face! You're lying!" she exclaimed.

For fuck sakes, if I didn't tell her, she'd never stop.

"We had sex in his bathroom," I spoke in a whisper.

"What did you say?" She walked up beside me and rested her hip on the counter.

"WE HAD SEX IN HIS BATHROOM!" I shouted.

She cupped her hand over her mouth in disbelief.

"Don't." I pointed at her. "Don't look at me with those judgy eyes!"

She immediately put her hands up.

"No judgment here. But, oh my god, I can't believe you did that. You don't even know him."

"Right." I nodded my head. "Like you should talk." I pointed at her.

"Hey. I own what I do. But it's what I've always done. You, on the other hand, have never fucked a guy you didn't know. In fact, they're lucky if you give in after the fifth date."

"I know." I lowered my head as I placed my hands on the sink and took in a breath. "I'm not proud of what I did. Believe me. It just happened."

She placed her hand on my back and began to softly rub it.

"Sometimes these things happen. He is definitely fuckable and gorgeous, so I don't blame you. Did you just leave his place after it happened?"

"Yes. I couldn't stay there."

"Did you at least exchange phone numbers?"

"He wanted it and I told him no. I said it was a one-time thing and it would never happen again."

"Good for you. #Delete without actually having to delete him." She smiled. "Don't overthink what happened." She kissed my head. "Chalk it up to a few moments of great sex and move along. You're far too busy to give it another thought."

"You're right." I sighed. "Already forgotten."

"Sure it is." She winked as she left my apartment.

After Natalie left, I grabbed a bottle of water from the refrigerator and retreated to my bedroom for the night. I plugged my phone in, set it on the nightstand, and climbed under the covers. As I lay there, my mind went into full replay mode about the events of tonight. I didn't want to rehash what had happened. I wanted to forget about it, but I couldn't. The sex was too good and so was Christian. He was the exact type of man I would fall in love with. I'd already felt the connection between us at Hellcat Annie's and, to be honest, my intuition wasn't saying a word to me. But men like him couldn't commit to one woman and he had proved that with the number of

#Delete

women he dated every week.

****

Christian

As hard as I tried to go on with the night and entertain my guests, I couldn't get Eloise out of my head. Maybe I shouldn't have had sex with her. Maybe I should have just stopped at the kiss. But she wasn't telling me to stop. Her body was perfection and the feeling I got while I was buried deep inside her was a feeling I'd never experienced before. *Shit.* I needed to apologize to her for what happened.

"Hey, Claire," I spoke as I lightly placed my hand on her shoulder. "Is there a chance you can give me Eloise's number?"

She looked at me in bewilderment.

"Umm. I'm sorry, Christian, but I can't. I can ask her if she wants me to give it to you."

"She won't. She already told me no tonight."

"Listen, she's been hurt recently. Not only recently, but a lot, and she's taking a step back from dating."

"I just want to take her out to dinner and maybe get to know her a little better."

"Dinner and getting to know someone usually equals a date, and that's something she doesn't want to do right now. She's got her career and that's what she's focusing on." She gave me a small, sympathetic smile.

"I understand." I nodded.

"Thanks for inviting me. I had a great time. I'll see you on

Monday," she spoke.

"Have a good weekend." I kissed her cheek.

After everyone cleared out and the caterers cleaned up and left, I headed to my bedroom. As I climbed into bed, I held my cellphone in my hand and pulled up my text messages. Was it too late to text Digits? It was midnight, but she did say she was out with friends.

"I hope it's not too late to text you."

"I'm awake," she replied with a smiley face.

"Did your evening get any better?"

"Not really. How about yours?"

"Could have been better."

"Something happen?"

"Nah. Just girl problems."

"Same here, but substitute the girl with a guy."

"Another douchebag?"

"I haven't decided yet. What's your girl problem? If you don't mind me asking?"

"She's just someone I want to get to know better."

"Then go after her. You do know it's the guy's job to chase the woman."

"She wants nothing to do with me."

"Then she's not worth the trouble of getting to know."

#Delete

"Perhaps you're right. I'll catch ya later, Digits. I'm tired. Good night."

"Catch ya later, Mobile Man. Good night."

Maybe Eloise wasn't worth the trouble, but I still needed to apologize to her.

Chapter Ten

Eloise

I turned off my alarm, stumbled out of bed, and made my way to the kitchen for a cup of coffee. I had hoped that sometime during the night, the sensation that flowed through my body from Christian would cease. But it didn't. After letting out a long yawn, I grabbed my coffee and headed to the bathroom for a shower and to get ready for the wedding I was shooting today. The thing I loved about Sunday weddings was the fact that they were always in the afternoon and over with by five o'clock.

After the ceremony and photo shoot with the bride, groom, and the bridal party, it was time to head to the reception at Antun's in Queens Village. As I was photographing the guests, I was startled when I heard a voice come up from behind him.

"Eloise?"

"Christian?"

My stomach twisted in a ball and a wave of heat swept over me as I turned around.

"You're photographing this wedding?" he asked.

"Yeah. What are you doing here?" I nervously asked.

"The groom is a friend of mine. Wow. I can't believe you're

#Delete

standing in front of me. I really need to talk to you. I tried to get your number from Claire, but she wouldn't give it to me."

"I'm sorry, but I'm really busy. I don't have time to talk," I nervously spoke as I needed to get away from him.

The humiliation I felt after the events of last night was overwhelming.

"After the wedding, then. It's important. Please."

"Christian, look—"

"Eloise, please," he softly spoke.

"Okay. Fine. After the wedding, but I only have a few minutes."

"A few minutes is all I need."

He gave me a small smile and walked away.

What could he possibly want to talk to me about? I could barely look him in the eye, let alone carry on a conversation with him. Once the wedding came to an end and I said goodbye to the bride and groom, I headed out the door and found Christian sitting on the edge of the retainer wall in front of the fountain. I took in a long, deep breath and walked over to him.

"Hey."

"Hi," he spoke as he stood up.

"So what did you want to talk to me about?" I nervously asked.

"I just wanted to apologize to you for last night. I shouldn't have come on so strong. It was wrong and I'm sorry."

Wait a minute. Was he actually apologizing for having sex with me?

I didn't know how to respond. No guy had ever done that before. It was at that moment that stupid fell from my mouth.

"Don't apologize. It's not like I tried to stop you. I was a willing partner."

"Still. It never should have happened and I just wanted to clear the air. I know how upset you were afterwards. And Claire is your friend, who happens to be an employee of mine. I'm sure we'll run into each other from time to time and I don't want there to be any awkwardness."

I sighed as I took a seat on the wall and he sat down next to me.

"It's not that I was upset, Christian. What happened is something I don't ever do."

"You don't ever have sex?" He smirked.

I let out a light laugh.

"I have sex, just not with a guy I don't know. Guys are lucky if I give it up on the fifth date."

"I respect that. You, Eloise, are a woman of value."

"Some value." I rolled my eyes.

"Shit happens. We've all made mistakes. Don't beat yourself up over it. I just wanted to apologize, that's all."

"Thank you. I appreciate it. But you seriously have no need to apologize."

#Delete

He got up from the wall and began to walk away. After placing his hands in his pockets, he stopped and slowly turned his head.

"For the record, I'm happy I was your first." He winked.

A small smile crossed my lips.

"For the record, I'm not considering it a mistake," I spoke.

He gave me a small smile and walked away. I already knew the kind of effect he had on women. It was the same effect I felt. Women fell hard and fast for him and if I gave him another thought, I would become one of those women. Hence the reason I couldn't get involved with him. I pulled my phone from my purse and sent a text message to Mobile Man.

"How's your day?"

"Funny, I was just thinking about texting you. Day turned out better than I thought it would. Yours?"

"It's good. Really good." I inserted a smiley face.

"Glad to hear. Any more dates scheduled?"

"Not yet, but I'm working on it." I sent the winky face.

"You'll find the right guy. I'm sure of it."

"I'm not looking for a guy or a relationship right now. Just some answers."

"??"

"I want to know a man's thought process when it comes to pursuing a woman."

"I'm not sure I understand."

69

"I want to know why they take hours or days to respond to a text message. Why do they suddenly go MIA or ghost a woman after leading her on?"

"I see. Maybe I can help you with that. We should meet for a drink." He inserted the smiley face.

"You're smooth, Mobile Man. But all is good. I'll get the information I need."

"So no drink?"

"No drink. Do you really want to ruin what we have by actually meeting each other? Don't you think this is fun? The two of us just randomly talking every day without knowing who the other is?"

"I will admit it's weird, Digits. But I'm cool with it. I like talking to you."

"I like talking to you too."

"One last question and then I have to go. How old are you?"

I didn't see the harm in telling him my age. Plus, it would be good to know his. What if he was some sixty-year-old man or something. Not that it would matter because I liked talking to him. But it would be kind of weird to carry on a texting relationship with someone that old.

"I'm twenty-five. And you?"

"Thirty."

Thank God. He was only a few years older than me.

"Have a good night, my friend," I replied.

#Delete

"You too, Digits. Be safe and behave yourself."

"You too. Don't go out and be a douchebag to some poor girl."

"I will keep my douchebaggery to a minimum."

I smiled as I closed out of my messages and placed my phone in my purse. It was time to go home, get changed, and hit up the bar to try and meet some guys.

Chapter Eleven

Christian

As much as I hated to admit it, I felt this incredibly strong connection to Eloise, a connection I had never felt before with any woman. Perhaps this was the connection I'd been searching for my entire dating life. Not only did I feel it the moment I laid eyes on her at Hellcat Annie's, or the moment we had sex in my bathroom, but sitting on the wall and talking to her made it even stronger. I couldn't explain it and I didn't want to think about it anymore. She wasn't interested in dating anyone, and as hard as it was, I needed to respect that. I wanted to know what happened in her last relationship and there was one person who could tell me.

The next morning, after grabbing some coffee and getting settled into work, I called Claire into my office.

"What's up, Christian?" She cheerfully smiled.

"Have a seat, please. I have a question about your friend Eloise."

She sat there with a narrowing eye.

"I'm not sure I can answer your question, but try me."

Leaning back in my chair and bringing my ankle up to my knee, I spoke, "What happened in her last relationship?"

#Delete

"Excuse me?" She cocked her head.

"I'm assuming he hurt her pretty bad. Bad enough that she doesn't want to date anyone right now."

"You mean date *you*, right?"

"Me or anyone else. Is it just *me* she doesn't want to date?" I cautiously asked.

"To put your mind at ease, Christian, no, it's not just you. Eloise doesn't want to date period. As for her last relationship, it wasn't even a real relationship. She and the guy had been talking for a few months, went out a couple of times, and then he decided they were getting too close. That was the straw that broke the camel's back for her. She's never been lucky in the relationship department. All the guys she attracts are total assholes."

I raised my brow at her. "Including me?"

"Oh, God, no. Of course not. It's just the timing of the two of you meeting was wrong."

"Yeah. Maybe it was. Thanks, Claire."

"Sure." She nodded with a small smile as she got up from her seat and walked out of my office.

I picked up a pen that was lying on my desk and started twirling it between my fingers. As much as I needed to respect her decision about not wanting to go out with me, giving up wasn't an option. To be honest, I didn't even know where the hell all this was coming from. I didn't chase women. They chased me. But Eloise was different. And even though I really didn't know her, she possessed something I couldn't explain.

Sandi Lynn

****

Eloise

I didn't get home until two a.m. Thank God, my photo shoot wasn't until eleven o'clock. Natalie and I hit up three different bars and I gave my number to three different guys. As I was sitting on the couch drinking my coffee and trying to wake up, my phone dinged with a text message from Mobile Man.

"Good morning. How did your quest go last night?"

"Good morning. Three different guys have become my victims. Now to patiently wait for the text messages to pour in."

"Good for you, tiger! Just wanted to check in. I have a busy day. Catch ya later?"

"I have a busy day as well. Catch ya later, Mobile Man."

After finishing my coffee, I headed into the bathroom to take a shower and get ready for my photo shoot. Today's shoot was for *Vibe* magazine, photographing their spring collection for next year. They had a regular photographer they used, but he had a family emergency and had been in Europe for the past month, so they called upon me to take his place until he came back. I had about thirty minutes until I needed to get ready to leave, so I opened my laptop and started to look for some other bars I could hit up tonight. While I was researching, an ad popped up for a singles mixer over at the Loews Hotel, which was being held tomorrow night. Why didn't I think of something like that sooner? My fingers started typing away in the Google search bar: Single Mixers in New York City. Jackpot! There was Date & Dash, Weekend Dating, Flirt Fete, Eight at Eight, and a lot more festivities around the city. Excitement overtook me. As much as I wanted my friends to go with me, I couldn't ask them since they were already in relationships. Except for Natalie, but she was getting ready to leave on a trip with her mom to Hawaii. So, I would be going solo.

I sent the models on a break about halfway into the shoot because I could tell they were getting tired and hungry. Pulling my phone from my purse, I noticed I had three text messages. All from the guys I met last night.

Frank: "Hi there! It was great meeting you last night. Are you free for dinner this week?"

Ron: "Eloise, it's Ron from last night. You up for a drink later?"

Mark: "Hi. It was great meeting you last night. Drinks and dinner sometime soon?"

I immediately replied to all three messages.

"Hi Frank, I'm available tomorrow night. Say seven o'clock at Tavern on the Green?"

If I played my cards right, I could squeeze in a drink with Ron and dinner with Mark in the same night.

Hi, Ron. Drinks tonight at Didjo's? Around six o'clock? I only have a couple of hours."

Ron: "I'll meet you there. A couple of hours is good to start. See you at six."

Hi, Mark. It was great meeting you too. I'm available tonight for dinner. Why don't we do Tavern on the Green at eight-thirty? That way, I'll have time to get ready after work."

Mark: "I can do tonight at eight-thirty. See you then."

I smiled as I closed out of my messages. See what I did there? I didn't give them a choice. I took control, which only gave them about ten seconds to think about it. If I would have let them choose the day, time, and place, it would have given them too much time to think and the possibility of a prompt date would have decreased.

After the photo shoot ended, I looked at my watch and it was five o'clock. It would take me at least a half hour to get home, which meant I only had about twenty minutes to get ready to meet Ron. As I was running the brush through my long brown hair, my phone dinged with a text message from Mobile Man.

"Good evening. How was your day?"

"Busy, but good. How was yours?" I asked.

"Also busy, but not too bad. Plans for tonight?"

"Actually, I have two dates."

"Two? What are you doing? Seeing them at the same time?"

"LOL. No. I have drinks with Ron at six and dinner with Mark at eight-thirty."

"Ah. You're quite the little lioness, going after her prey. I sort of feel sorry for these guys."

"They'll be fine. It's all in the name of research."

"I can still help you with your research. Where are you meeting this Ron guy for drinks?"

"Wouldn't you love to know? The last thing I'd need is you coming up to us and telling him how you're the guy I text every single day."

"It would be fun, though."

"What are you doing tonight?"

"Going to a strip club for my friend's thirtieth birthday."

"Ah, lots of tits and ass for you tonight."

"I guess so." He sent the winky face. *"Have fun on your dates tonight. I need to jump in the shower."*

"I will. Thanks. You too. Do me a favor and don't pay extra to have sex with one of those strippers. God knows what you'll catch."

"Lol. I wouldn't touch any of them anyway. They aren't my type. Catch ya later, Digits."

"Catch ya later, Mobile Man."

Chapter Twelve

Eloise

Drinks with Ron was interesting and dinner with Mark was very informative. Both seemed like nice guys. I didn't want to overload them with questions right off the bat, so I discreetly snuck them in when the opportunity was right. By time I made it home, it was eleven thirty and I was exhausted.

Kicking off my heels the minute I stepped inside my apartment, I went straight to my bedroom and changed into my nightshirt. The whole time I was with those guys, Christian wormed his way into my mind. In fact, he was on my mind more than he should have been. It wasn't just the sex I kept thinking about, it was the conversation we had after the wedding and the way he apologized to me. Does a man even do that? He did and he was sincere. I sensed it and I could tell by his body language and his tone. Maybe giving him a chance wouldn't be so bad? No. No way. I wasn't ready to go down that road again.

I grabbed my laptop and climbed into bed. After getting myself situated, I decided to check my email for my blog. My eyes just about popped out of my head when I saw that I had over a hundred messages from the past couple of days from women asking relationship questions and seeking answers. As I was reading a few of them over, my phone dinged with a text message from Mobile Man.

#Delete

"I know it's late and I'm sorry. How did your dates go?"

"It's okay. I'm still up. They were very informative. How was the strip club?"

"Like any other strip club. I want to meet you, Digits."

"You're drunk, Mobile Man."

"Maybe a little. Okay, maybe a lot. I think I'm drunk texting you."

"Go to sleep and we'll chat tomorrow."

I waited for a reply that never came. He must have passed out. Rolling my eyes, I continued to read a couple more emails before drifting off to sleep.

****

The next morning as I was sitting on the couch editing some wedding photos, my phone dinged with a text message from Claire.

"Lunch today?"

"Sure. What time?"

"Noon. Come to the advertising agency and pick me up."

"I don't think that's such a good idea."

"Why?"

"Because I really don't want to run into Christian."

"He won't be here. He has a client meeting across town at eleven thirty."

"Okay. Send me the address and I'll see you at noon."

As I was sitting in the back of the cab on my way to pick up Claire, I decided to send Mobile Man a text message.

"How's the hangover?"

"How do you know I'm hungover?"

"You celebrated a birthday at a strip club. You're hungover."

"You're right and I'm sorry I didn't respond last night. I passed out."

"I figured. Did you bring home any strippers with you?"

"Nah. None of them were interested." He sent the winky face.

"Why? Were you using your douchebaggery moves on them?"

"I'm not sure. I don't remember, lol."

As soon as the cab pulled up to the curb of 276 5th Avenue, I paid the fare, climbed out, and stepped into the forty-one-story building. Taking the elevator up to the thirtieth floor, I stepped out and was greeted by a young blonde woman with bright red lips.

"Good afternoon, welcome to Blake Group. How may I help you?" She proudly smiled.

"Hi. I'm here to see Claire—"

Before I could get her last name out, I heard her voice coming from the opposite way.

"Good, you're here. Just give me a second while I grab my

purse." She smiled.

She walked past me and I glanced down at my phone, replying to Christian's text message.

"You probably didn't offer them enough money." I sent the smiley face.

"I hope not. I'm usually a very generous guy."

I let out a light laugh.

"So you pay top dollar for sex?"

"Sweetheart, I don't have to pay for sex. Woman give it up to me for free."

I smiled, and as I looked up to see if Claire was coming, I saw Christian heading toward me with his phone in his hand.

"Eloise. What a nice surprise." He smiled.

My stomach started to flip in a million different ways, causing an overwhelming nervousness to erupt.

"Hi, Christian."

"How are you?" he asked as his eyes stared into mine.

"I'm good. And you?"

"Good. Are you here for Claire?"

"Umm. Yeah. We're going to lunch."

"Have a nice lunch." He smiled. "I have a meeting across town I have to get to. It was good seeing you again, Eloise."

"You too, Christian." I politely smiled.

"You ready?" Claire asked as she walked up.

"You told me he wouldn't be here!" I spoke through gritted teeth as I hooked my arm around hers.

"His meeting just got pushed back right before you got here. I didn't have time to warn you. By the way, what the hell is going on?"

"What do you mean?"

We stepped out of the building and walked down to Ai Fiori because Claire was in the mood for Italian.

"Why are you behaving like that towards Christian? I really don't understand it at all. I mean, I know he asked for your number and he's interested in you, but you don't have to avoid him like the plague. I already told him that you've been hurt a lot and you're stepping away from the dating scene for a while."

"What?! When did you tell him that?"

"The Monday after his party. He called me into his office and wanted to know about your previous relationship. Oops. Maybe I shouldn't have told you that." She bit down on her bottom lip.

"And you told him that I have had nothing but one failed relationship after another?" I narrowed my eye at her.

"I didn't say that. I just said you haven't been lucky in the relationship department."

"Ugh. Claire!"

"What?"

I swallowed hard because I was about to tell her that I slept with her boss. I wasn't sure how she was going to take it, but she had to know.

"We fucked in his bathroom."

She let out a roaring laugh.

"I'm sorry, I swear you just said you and Christian fucked in his bathroom."

I lowered my head and didn't say a word.

"What the fuck, Eloise! Is that why you ran out of there so fast?"

I slowly nodded my head.

"How the hell did that happen and where was I? Oh my God, you slept with my boss!"

"It just did. He showed me where the bathroom was upstairs and then he was waiting for me when I was done. It just happened and believe me, I'm still in shock at myself for letting it. But, I ran into him the next day at the wedding I was photographing and he apologized to me."

"Apologized? For what? Having sex with you?"

"Yes."

"What man does that?" Her brows furrowed. "Listen, Eloise, you know I love you to pieces and I totally respect what you're doing for your blog, but maybe you should give Christian a chance. There's obviously a strong connection between the two of you."

"And look at where connections have gotten me before. That doesn't mean shit, Claire. Yes, two people can have a connection, but it doesn't stop men from being jerks. It all comes down to a woman's self-worth and value, and the more women put up with men behaving badly, the lower their self-esteem gets. We shouldn't have to play games or be put through the ringer with these guys."

"I agree. But maybe, just a small maybe," she pinched her fingers together, "Christian is different. You could always just try him and then #Delete his ass. Isn't that what you're promoting?"

"Yes. But I'm not in any position right now to even be thinking about #Deleting someone. I'm far too busy with the blog and my work. Oh shit." I pulled my phone from my purse.

"What?" Claire asked.

"Hold on. I have to send a text back to Mobile Man."

She sighed and rolled her eyes as she sipped her glass of wine.

"Actually, it does cost you. You take them to dinner, drinks, and maybe a movie. That costs money. So the sex isn't totally free, darling."

"I was starting to think I scared you off."

"Lol, sorry. I'm out and about. I'm sure you're busy with work. Catch ya later?"

"Catch ya later, Digits."

"FOCUS!" Claire loudly voiced as she pointed to herself.

#Delete

Chapter Thirteen

Christian

Focusing on my meeting was hard since I saw Eloise standing in the lobby of my firm. She looked as beautiful as ever and the moment I saw her, that night in my bathroom started to play in my mind. I couldn't forget her. No matter how hard I tried, she was always in my head.

When I arrived back to the office, I walked over to Claire's cubicle and asked how her lunch was.

"It was good, Christian," she spoke as she gave me a strange look.

"Good. I'm happy to hear that." I tucked my hands in my pants pockets.

"Is that all?" she asked as she cocked her head.

"Yeah." I nodded.

I walked away and went into my office. Pulling my phone from my pocket, I noticed I had a text message from Victoria.

"Hey, handsome. I haven't heard from you in a few days. Are we still on for tonight?"

Shit. I totally forgot I had set up a date with her.

"Hi. Sorry about that. Work has been crazy. Yes, we are still on for tonight. Why don't we meet at Tavern on the Green at seven o'clock?"

"Sounds lovely. I'll see you then."

Sighing, I set my phone down and turned to my computer.

"What was that sigh for?" Peter asked as he walked into my office.

"A date I forgot I set up for tonight."

"Who's the lucky girl?" He smirked as he took a seat across from my desk.

"Victoria."

"Isn't she the chick you met that night at the art gallery?"

"No. That was someone else."

He slowly shook his head. "Dude, I can't keep up. What happened with the art gallery chick?"

"Nothing. We had dinner and I couldn't get away from her fast enough. She was annoying."

Just as Peter was going to say something, my phone dinged with a text message. Glancing over at it, I looked at Peter.

"Great. It's her." I rolled my eyes.

"You said you were going to call me and I'm still waiting. What is going on? I thought our dinner went well. I thought we connected. Why haven't you called me for another date?"

"Well," Peter spoke. "What did she say?"

#Delete

"She wants to know why I didn't call her like I said I was going to."

"Don't respond. I hate chicks like that."

"It would be rude of me not to. I'll just simply tell her that I've been busy with work."

"Bro, if you do that, then she'll be all up your ass. Silence is a better form of rejection."

"I guess you're right. I don't have time to deal with her anyway." I set my phone down.

"Still thinking about that Eloise girl?" he asked. "I saw her in the lobby earlier. What was she doing here?"

"She was meeting Claire for lunch."

"I know what your problem is." He pointed at me. "You're so enthralled with her because she turned you down. You want what you can't have."

"That's not true, Peter. I'm attracted to her in a way I have never been attracted to any other woman before."

"Because she turned you down." He cocked his head.

It wasn't worth arguing with him over it. He was going to believe what he wanted to, so I just decided to go along with it.

"Yeah. Maybe you're right. Maybe the appeal to her is because she turned me down."

"There you go, man." He pointed at me as he got up from his seat. "Now forget about her and enjoy your date with Victoria tonight."

I gave him a small smile as he exited my office.

****

Eloise

When I returned home, I set my purse on the table, grabbed my laptop, and resumed editing the wedding photos before I had to get ready for my date with Frank. As I was diligently working, my phone dinged with a text message from him.

"Hey, I'm not going to be able to make our date tonight. Something came up. Another time?"

I sat there and glared at the text message before me. His lack of explanation and only stating "something came up" was a lie. And his "another time" was code for "we aren't ever going on a date." But I decided to play along and see what exactly this asshole was up to.

"Bummer. I was looking forward to seeing you, but I totally understand. Things come up all the time. When are you free again?"

"I may be available Thursday night. I'll have to check my schedule and get back with you."

"Okay. I'm free Thursday. If you can't do dinner, maybe we can meet for lunch."

"I'll check it out and let you know. Again, I'm sorry I had to cancel tonight."

"No problem."

My ass he was sorry and I could guarantee that I wouldn't hear from him again. I went back to editing the photos when my phone dinged again. This time, it was from a number I didn't recognize. Opening the text, I rolled my eyes as I read it.

"What's up?"

"What's up is me wondering who this is?" I replied.

"Really? It's Eddie."

Ah, Eddie Fischer. The guy whom I hadn't heard from for approximately eight months. The same guy who took me out on four dates, constantly text messaged me, and then—*poof*—disappeared without a trace, AKA ghosted me.

"I thought you died." I smiled as I hit the send button.

"Lol. Why would you think that?"

"Gee, I don't know, maybe because it's been eight months since I've heard from you. I figured you got into some kind of accident and were buried six feet under."

"That's weird, Eloise. I've been really busy with work. I started a new position that took up all of my time."

"Good for you, Eddie. So why are you texting me?"

"I thought maybe we could meet up for dinner and a movie; resume getting to know each other better."

"That's nice of you, but the time to get to know each other better has expired. Bye."

I smiled as I deleted his text message and continued with my work. After I finished with the last photo, I went into the kitchen to throw something together for dinner. While I was cutting up some vegetables for a stir fry and listening to some music on my phone, a text message came through from Mobile Man.

"Getting ready for your date?"

"My wonderful date cancelled on me, so I'm just going to enjoy a nice quiet evening at home."

"He sucks. Why did he cancel?"

"He claims something came up."

"Ouch. That usually indicates he changed his mind or got a better offer."

"I know. We're supposed to set up something for Thursday, but I doubt I'll hear from him again."

"I'm sorry." He sent the sad face emoji.

"Don't be. I was only using him for research anyway. I'm just going to make myself a stir fry for dinner and do some work."

"I like stir fry. Maybe I can come over and keep you and your stir fry company." He sent the winky face.

"I'm my own good company. But thanks for the offer. What are your plans for tonight?"

"I have a date."

"Sounds like fun. Who's the lucky lady?"

"It could be a girl I call Digits, but she refuses to meet me, so I have to settle for a woman named Victoria."

"Lol. I'm sure you'll have a nice time."

"Perhaps. I'll catch ya later, Digits."

"Don't be a douchebag, Mobile Man. Catch ya later."

#Delete

    I smiled as I set my phone down on the counter and continued cooking my stir fry.

Chapter Fourteen

Christian

I sat on the edge of my bed staring down at my phone. I couldn't stop thinking about Eloise. I pulled up Victoria's number and gave her a call.

"Hello," she answered.

"Victoria, it's Christian. I'm stuck at work with a huge problem, so I'm going to have to cancel our date for tonight. I'm sorry."

"Damn you, Christian. I was really looking forward to seeing you."

"I know and I'm sorry. It can't be helped."

"I understand. Call me soon and we'll set something up."

"I will, and thanks for understanding, Victoria. I'll be in touch."

"No problem. Just don't take as long next time."

"Have a good night."

"You too, Christian."

I let out a sigh of relief and sent a text message to Digits.

#Delete

"How about a text date tonight?"

"Huh?" She sent the confused face.

"We talk over text for a few hours. Unless you have a lot of work to do."

"I thought you had a date with Victoria?"

"I cancelled."

"Why?"

"I didn't feel like going out tonight."

"So you lied to her and told her something came up?"

"I told her I'm held up at the office with a problem."

"That was a douchebag move, Mobile Man."

"I know, but you don't understand. I can't stop thinking about this other woman and it wouldn't be fair to lead Victoria on."

"I guess I understand, but then you need to tell Victoria that. You need to be upfront and honest."

"So what do you want me to do?"

"Text her and tell her and then send me screenshots as proof. After you do that, I will have a text date with you." She sent the smiley emoji.

"Are you serious?"

"Very."

"Fine. Just give me a few minutes."

"Waiting…"

I couldn't believe what I was about to do. And for what? A few hours of text talk with a girl I'd never even met? Digits was worth it, though. I enjoyed talking to her for some odd reason, and tonight, I wanted to spend an evening with her, even if it was just over text messaging.

I sent Victoria a message telling her that I lied and something didn't come up. I explained how it wouldn't be fair to lead her on. She called me every name in the book and then told me to lose her number. I took a screenshot of the conversation and sent it to Digits.

"Happy?"

"Actually, I am, Mobile Man. That was very noble of you to come clean. Very mature as far as I'm concerned."

"Our text date will begin at nine o'clock. I'm going to grab some dinner first. Unless you have some of that stir fry left?"

"Sorry, I ate it all. I'll be anxiously waiting for your text. Catch ya later, Mobile Man."

"Catch ya later, Digits."

I smiled as I got up from the bed and headed down to the kitchen.

Chapter Fifteen

Eloise

After cleaning up the kitchen, I looked at the time on my phone and saw it was seven o'clock. I had two hours before my text date with Mobile Man, so I decided to pour a glass of wine and take a relaxing bubble bath. While I was running my hands through the bubbly water, a text message came through on my phone from Natalie.

"I know you're on your date, but I wanted to tell you I met a guy and he's dreamy."

"Frank cancelled. Something came up. Who is this guy? Send me a pic."

"Fuck Frank! I'm sorry he cancelled. His name is Nathan and he's from Long Island. Small world, eh?"

"Age?"

"He's thirty-seven and an architect. Believe it or not, he seems to have his shit together. He's never been married, owns his own home, and he has a cat named Lucy. He taught me how to surf."

"Aw, Nat, that's great. I still want a pic."

"So what are you doing tonight since fucker Frank

cancelled?"

"Mobile Man and I are having a text date."

"Huh? What do you mean?"

"We're both staying home and texting each other."

"Okay, seriously, Eloise, you've hit rock bottom. Just fucking meet the guy already. Go on a real date."

"Nah, and I haven't hit rock bottom. I don't want to ruin our friendship by meeting him. We have a cool thing going on."

"I have to go. My mom and I are heading to lunch, but we're going to have a long talk when I get back. So prepare yourself."

"Yes, Ma'am. Enjoy your day!"

I set my phone down and closed my eyes, taking in the hot bubbly water that soothed my skin. As I was feeling like I was drifting away to another world, my phone dinged. Opening one eye, I glanced over at it and stared at the number carefully. It was Luke.

"Hey, I know you don't want to talk to me, but I really want to talk to you. I'm not comfortable with the way we left things in our last text. I do like you, Eloise. It's just I'm confused."

I let out a laugh as I read his text. Was he serious?

"You have a lot of balls texting me. Too bad you didn't have those balls while we were seeing each other. Let me un-confuse you. You led me on, made me think that you were interested in me, we flirted, we kissed, and then poof, you disappeared and proceeded to give me a speech on how you felt we were getting too close and you needed to focus on you and the kids. You never should have pursued me the way you did knowing you

#Delete

didn't want to date. But you did and you hurt me. I can forgive, but I will never forget. You're a breadcrumber who needs an ego boost every once in a while, and I'm not the woman to give you one. You do not deserve my attention or my words. In fact, you don't even deserve these words, but you're getting them so you'll leave me the hell alone. You have been #deleted and it's going to stay that way. You don't have the right to pop in and out of people's lives when it suits you."

"I'm sorry and I understand. It appears you've given up on me."

"Your time has expired. Take care and I hope you get your life straightened out."

Good lord, he was an idiot. For someone his age, it bewildered me how unintelligent he was. What was with tonight? Return of the exes? I turned my phone off so I could enjoy the rest of my bath in peace. After changing into my pajamas, I grabbed a bottle of wine from the kitchen and took it over to the couch. I had approximately thirty minutes before my text date with Mobile Man started, so I opened my lap top and read some more emails from women all over the world with relationship questions. Starting tomorrow, I would make daily blog posts answering the questions they had. As I was reading over the emails, my phone dinged with a message from Frank. With an arch in my brow, I read his text message.

"Hey, I'm free now if you want to still meet up."

"Really? I thought something came up?"

"It did, but I resolved it, so now I'm free."

"I take it your other date stood you up?"

"What? Umm. No. Of course not. Why would you say that?"

"Listen, Frank. I'm not stupid, so just come clean with me. The sooner you do, the sooner we can wipe the slate clean and maybe start over."

"Fine. I'm sorry, Eloise. I did lie to you. I met this girl this morning at a coffee shop and I asked her out and the only time she had available was tonight."

"Go on..."

"We were supposed to meet at eight o'clock for dinner, but she called and said she changed her mind. She said something about she's not over her ex yet."

"So you benched me to go out with her, and if it didn't work out, you felt you could always set up another date with me?"

"I guess I did. I'm sorry. Can we still go out? I really like you."

"If you did REALLY like me, you wouldn't have cancelled to go out with some chick from the coffee shop you just met today. Our time to get to know each other expired when you cancelled our date and failed to give me an explanation. Just for future reference, Frank, women don't like the 'something came up' excuse. I am now going to delete your number from my phone, so please don't text me again. In fact, don't even respond to this text. I've said my peace."

I threw my phone down on the couch, took a sip of my wine, and continued looking over the emails I received. It was eight fifty-five when my phone dinged with a text message from Mobile Man.

"Hi there. How are you?"

"Hi. You're five minutes early for our date."

#Delete

"I like to be a little early than late. Being late for something is just rude."

I couldn't help but smile.

"You sound like me. I can't stand being late for anything. My girlfriends, on the other hand, are opposite. My cancelled date resurrected and sent me a text message telling me that he's free now if I wanted to still go out."

"His other plans fell through I'm assuming."

"He met a girl at a coffee shop this morning and benched me to go with her. Silly boy for thinking that I'd still be waiting around."

"Benched you?"

"When a guy puts a girl on the bench to see if something better is out there. Kind of like keeping her in the wings. It's comparable to when a basketball coach benches one of his not-so-great players to play the really good ones."

"I see. I didn't know there was a word for that. He actually told you that he met a girl today at the coffee shop?"

"Yes. I made him."

I took a screenshot of our conversation and sent it to Mobile Man.

"Damn, Digits, you really told him. I'm impressed."

"Thank you." I sent the smiley face emoji.

Chapter Sixteen

Christian

Digits was fierce and I couldn't help but be a little turned on by her self-confidence. I needed to; no, I wanted to get to know her better.

"Have you always lived in New York?" I asked.

"Yes. And you?"

"Yes. Do you have any other fierce siblings out in the world?"

"No. I'm an only child. My parents tried for years after I was born, but my mom couldn't conceive."

"I'm an only child as well. My parents didn't even want children to begin with, but accidents happen. Are your parents still married?"

"Yes. They have the best relationship ever. My dad is a one-of-a-kind guy, and so far, every guy I've met doesn't even come close to him."

"So you're searching for someone like your father?"

"He's a good guy who loves my mom very much. He's never lied to her, cheated on her, and they barely argue. It would be nice to have a guy like that in my life."

"Sounds abnormal to me."

"It's how I was raised, so my standards are set pretty high. What about your parents?"

"My dad passed away a few years ago and my mom has since gotten married to someone else."

"I'm sorry for your loss. It's nice that your mom moved on. Do you like him?"

"Thanks. Yes, I do. He's a good guy and treats her well. What's your favorite type of food?"

"Italian. Unfortunately, I love all those carbs."

"Lol. Me too. But I get the impression you stay fit."

"I do. Now back to relationships. Why don't you have a girlfriend? You seem like a nice guy without too much douchebaggery going on."

"I've had a couple of relationships in my life, but they didn't seem to work out. I was busy with my work and it pretty much consumed all my time. I guess it's just easier to date a variety of women without all the drama and hassles of a relationship."

"A person is never too busy when they find the right person, Mobile Man."

"Then maybe I just haven't found the right woman yet."

"What about that girl you were telling me about? The one who doesn't want to get to know you?"

"She's one I definitely can't stop thinking about."

"What's so special about her?"

"She's beautiful and kind. I don't know how to explain it, Digits. There's just something about her."

"Does she have a boyfriend or something?"

"No. She just got out of a relationship and isn't ready to date anyone yet."

"I can relate to that. If you want my opinion, I think you should chase her. Make her want to get to know you."

"Isn't that a fine line of stalking?"

"No, lol. Women love to be chased by men. Just don't be creepy about it, and whatever you do, don't be a douchebag! Unless she totally despises you. Does she despise you?"

"I don't think so. She gets really nervous around me. I think she wants to go out but is afraid. From what I understand, she's been hurt in the past."

"Again, I can relate. Everybody's been hurt by someone. If you really can't stop thinking about her, then do something different to grab her attention."

"Like what?"

"I don't know. Try to get to know her better without asking her on a date. Make it something totally casual."

"Good idea. I'll give it some thought. So, what about you? What's on the dating horizon for my friend Digits?"

"You already know, Mobile Man."

"Ah, that's right. You're just trying to get inside the heads *of men. What did you say you do again?"*

"I'm in social media relations."

"Too vague for me, darling. I don't quite understand."

"I'm a writer and I'm helping women with relationship advice for men who behave badly."

"Huh? What do you mean 'men who behave badly'?"

"Guys who ghost, bench, breadcrumb, zombie, etc."

"LOL! Come on! What the hell does all that mean?"

"Have you ever disappeared from a woman's life without any explanation? Just cut off all contact abruptly because you didn't feel like seeing her anymore? Be honest, Mobile Man."

"Well, yes, I have."

"You ghosted that poor girl. You already know what benching is because I explained what happened to me tonight. Now, have you ever dated someone a couple of times but aren't really feeling it but don't want to cut ties off completely in case you get bored or lonely? Did you ever just randomly text that girl, throwing out little nibbles of I'm interested still so please don't go anywhere?"

"Maybe."

"You are a breadcrumber, Mobile Man."

"You're being ridiculous, Digits."

"If you don't believe me, look it up for yourself."

"So what the fuck is a zombie?"

"*After you ghosted a woman, have you ever come back, like six months later and out of nowhere text her and ask what's up?*"

"*Jesus, Digits.*"

"*I'll take that as a yes. Zombie-ing is when the ghoster returns after a period of time. They rise from the dead, so I like to say.*"

"*I just want to set the record straight. Once I'm done with a woman, I don't go back. So, no, I do not zombie. Maybe the others, but not that.*"

"*I take great comfort in knowing you've done the others but not that one, lol.*"

"*Let me get this straight, you're saying that only men do it and women don't do this shit?*"

"*No. I know women do it, but I'm helping the ones get away from the men who do it.*"

"*Good luck with that. I think every man does it.*"

"*Only the ones who haven't found the right woman to share their life with. And the ones who are seriously fucked in the head and don't deserve a woman in their life period.*"

"*Do you think I'm fucked in the head?*"

"*No, lol. I just think you haven't found the right woman yet. In fact, I wonder if this girl you can't stop thinking about is the one for you.*"

"*Guess only time will tell. I'm going to take your advice and chase her. No matter what, I will get her to go out with me.*"

#Delete

"That's the spirit, Mobile Man. I'm proud of you. It's getting late and I'm tired. Chat tomorrow?"

"Of course. This was fun, Digits."

"It was!"

"I still think we should meet?"

"And ruin this fun we have? I like it better this way. Good night, Mobile Man."

"Good night, Digits. Sleep well."

I set my phone down and sighed. Talking to her had become the best part of my day. As weird and strange as it sounded, I felt like she was becoming my best friend. How would I explain that to people?

Chapter Seventeen

Eloise

It had been a long and exhausting day with back to back photo shoots: A socialite who held a charity event at her house in the afternoon, and a couple's twenty-fifth wedding anniversary at night. By the time I got home, it was late and all I wanted to do was collapse in bed and drift off into dreamland. After washing my face and changing into my pajamas, I picked up my phone from my bed and saw I had a text message from Ron.

"Hey there, sexy girl. Let's do dinner tomorrow night."

"Hi, Ron. I have plans tomorrow night. How's Tuesday night look for you?"

"I'm leaving for out of town on Tuesday. I really wanted to see that beautiful smile before I left. Cancel your plans and have dinner with me."

"I can't. I'm sorry. But I am free for lunch if you want to meet up."

"Why do you have to be so difficult? Just cancel your plans."

For fuck sakes, was this guy serious? #Delete on the way.

"The answer is no! I do not cancel my plans for anyone.

Especially for someone I've only had drinks with for a couple of hours. If this is the way you talk to women on a regular basis, it's no wonder why you're single."

"Forget I even asked. You aren't worth any more of my time."

Rolling my eyes, I deleted his number from my phone. I was way too tired to deal with this bullshit from anyone. There was one thing I needed to do before I went to sleep.

"Hi. Sorry it took me so long to respond to your last text message. It's been a very long and exhausting day."

"It's okay. I figured you were busy. Are you all right?"

"I'm fine. Just tired. How are you?"

"I'm good. Putting a plan into action for a meeting tomorrow." He sent the winky face. "I won't keep you. Get some rest, Digits, and sleep well. Good night. Catch ya later!"

"Good night, Mobile Man. Sweet dreams. Catch ya later!"

I always felt good after talking with Mobile Man. We were growing closer via text and as much as he wanted us to meet, I couldn't bring myself to. I loved what we had and I was too afraid that if we met, everything would go to shit and that was something I couldn't risk. I didn't believe a man and woman could just be friends.

****

I was doing my last photo shoot for the week, which was good because it would allow me to finish up previous edits and allow me to dive into my blog full-time. When I finished, I pulled my phone from my purse and noticed I had a missed call and text message from Claire. Dialing her number, I brought my phone up to my ear.

"Hello," she answered.

"Hey, you called?"

"Where are you?"

"I was doing a photo shoot all morning. Why?"

"Christian asked me to call you. He has a freelance job offer for you and would like you to come into the office if you're interested."

"Doing what?" I asked.

"Photography, I'm assuming. Can you come in now?"

"I don't know, Claire. I don't think it's a good idea."

"Eloise, it's a job and I'm sure it pays well. You'd be a fool not to at least listen to him."

"I guess. I'm not too far. I'll head over there now."

"Great. I'll let him know."

I put my phone back in my purse and hailed a cab over to Christian's advertising firm. Why on earth would he offer me a job? Was he doing this purely for ulterior motives? But photographing for an advertising firm, especially his that was on the rise, could mean bigger and better things for me.

When I arrived at his office, I found Claire, who took me to see Christian. The moment I stepped through the double glass doors, he stood up from behind his desk with a panty-melting smile on his face.

#Delete

"Thank you for coming, Eloise. Please, have a seat."

"Hello, Christian." I politely smiled. "Now what's this about the freelance job Claire told me about?" I asked as I took a seat across from his desk and tightly crossed my legs to try and stop the vibrating sensation I felt below.

"I need a photographer. Our current photographer, Max, is out sick with pneumonia and we have a perfume shoot coming up at the end of the week. You were the first person I thought of." He smirked.

"Which perfume company?" I asked.

"It's for Chanel."

"Chanel? Are you freaking kidding me? How did you score that?"

He chuckled and leaned back in his chair.

"I have a good friend who is one of the V.P.'s. They were having some issues with their other firm, so he called me up and asked if we'd be interested. If the campaign goes well, he'll bring us on board for all Chanel campaigns and advertising."

"Wow. Talk about pressure." I inhaled a sharp breath. "You haven't even seen any of my work. How do you know I'm Chanel worthy?"

The corners of his mouth curved up into a sweet smile.

"I have faith in you. But I will need to see some of your work just to make sure." He winked.

"Of course. I don't have anything with me right now."

"That's okay. I can come with you back to your apartment

and I can have a look."

"You mean right now?"

"Yes. Right now." He looked at his Louis Vuitton watch, which sat proudly on his wrist. "In fact, it's almost dinner time. We can grab something on the way."

A nervousness settled inside me and my foot began to involuntarily tap on the floor. Chanel was too good of an opportunity to turn down. *Shit.* This would be the biggest shoot of my life.

"Okay. I don't have anything else going on tonight," I lied.

I was supposed to go to a singles mixer in the Fashion District, but that would have to wait for another time.

"Excellent. We can leave now if you're ready," Christian spoke as he got up from his chair.

"I am." I smiled. "Can I use your restroom before we head out?"

"Of course. Let me show you where it is."

I placed my hand on his muscular chest.

"Just point me in the right direction. Remember what happened last time you showed me where your restroom was?"

"How could I forget?" He slyly smiled.

We walked out of his office and he pointed down the hallway.

"Thank you." I nodded. "I'll be right back."

"You're welcome." He tucked his hands into his pants

pockets.

As soon as I entered the bathroom, I pulled my phone from my purse and sent a text message to Claire.

"I'm in the bathroom. Get in here now!"

"I'm on my way. Which bathroom are you in?"

"I don't know. The one down the hall from Christian's office."

"Oh okay. I'll be there in a sec."

I placed my hands on the sink and stared at myself in the mirror. Christian was coming over to my apartment, which didn't settle right with me. Being alone with him shouldn't be hard, but it would be. Especially after what happened that night at his party. The night that had been playing over and over in my mind since. The bathroom door opened and Claire walked in.

"What's going on?" she asked.

"Christian is coming over to my apartment to look at my portfolio."

"Okay? And?"

I grabbed her arms.

"Did you not hear me correctly? Christian is coming over to my place!"

"I heard you. So what? Are you afraid of him or something?"

I placed my hands on my head and scrunched my hair.

"Oh. I know what this is about," she spoke. "You're afraid

to be alone with him because you might have sex with him again."

"No." I wiggled my finger in front of her face. "I am not having sex with him again."

"Eloise." She sighed. "You know why you're not going to have sex with him again?"

"Because I said so?" I arched my brow.

"No. Christian won't make that mistake again. He already apologized to you for last time and he's not stupid enough to try it again."

"I guess you're right." I leaned against the sink.

"I am right. Now go and show Christian your portfolio. This is all strictly business."

I sighed. "Okay. Just give me a minute."

As soon as Claire left the bathroom, I pulled out my phone and sent a text message to Mobile Man.

"I just wanted to say hi."

"Hi." He sent the smiley face. *"Busy day today?"*

"Yes. How's your day going?"

"I can honestly say my day is fantastic."

"I'm happy to hear that. I have to go. I'm still working. Catch ya later?"

"Catch ya later, Digits."

#Delete

Chapter Eighteen

Eloise

When I opened the door to the bathroom, Christian was leaning against the wall.

"I thought maybe you fell in." He grinned.

"Very funny." I scrunched up my nose at him and he chuckled.

"What are you hungry for?" he asked.

"Pizza?" I bit down on my bottom lip.

"Pizza sounds good to me. How about Pizzapopulous? I can call it in now and it should be ready by time we get there."

"I love that place."

"Me too." He smiled. "What kind of pizza do you like?"

"Any kind really. Hawaiian, barbeque chicken, Mediterranean, or one with everything on it except anchovies."

"Ah, you're an everything on it kind of girl. I like that."

After picking up the pizza, we headed back to my apartment. My belly was doing backflips all the way there and it was pissing me off. Once we stepped inside my apartment, Christian set the pizza box on the kitchen counter and I grabbed a couple of paper plates and napkins.

"I have beer," I spoke.

"A beer sounds good. How many pieces of pizza do you want?"

"Two," I replied as I opened the fridge and grabbed two bottles of beer.

We both took a seat at my small round table for two and Christian popped the cap off his beer and took a sip while I bit into my pizza. The silence between us was eerie. It was almost as if either one of us was afraid to say something.

"As soon as we're done, I'll get my portfolio."

"I can't wait to see your work," he spoke as his eyes wandered around my apartment. "Your apartment is nice."

"Thanks." I gave him a small smile.

"Tell me a little bit about your family," he spoke.

"Why do you want to know about my family?"

"Why not?" He shrugged. "Would you rather talk about something else?"

"No. It's just me, my mom and my dad."

"You're an only child?"

"Yeah. My parents tried for years after I born, but my mom couldn't conceive."

"Ah, that's too bad. Are your parents still married?"

#Delete

"Yes." I smiled. "They have the best relationship ever. My dad is a one-of-a-kind guy."

****

Christian

I sat across from her with a bewildered look on my face. Those words. I'd heard them before. My mind started racing at such an uncontrollable speed, I couldn't keep up. Nah. Couldn't be. It had to be a coincidence. Doesn't every girl think her father is a one-of-a-kind guy?

"That's good to hear you think so highly about him. Tell me more."

"He's a good guy who loves my mom very much. He's never lied to her, cheated on her, and they barely argue. I can only count maybe two times my entire life where they got into a disagreement." She smiled.

My stomach twisted in a tight knot.

"Your standards for a guy must be pretty high then," I spoke.

"They are. Very high." She held up her beer bottle before tipping it to her lips.

"What's your favorite type of food?" I asked as I narrowed my eye at her.

"Italian. Unfortunately, I love all those carbs."

Holy shit. She can't be. This was all a coincidence. I gave her a small, nervous smile.

"I need to use your bathroom."

"Oh sure. It's down the hall, first door on the right." She pointed.

"I'll be right back."

I had to know for sure and there was only one way I could be certain. I stood around the corner, pulled my phone from my pocket, turned the sound off, and sent a text message to Digits.

"I hope your evening is going well."

I heard her phone ding and she got up from the table and took it from the kitchen counter.

"It is. How's yours?"

My phone lit up with a reply from her and my heart started racing.

"Good. Really good. Are you still working?" I hit the send button.

Her phone dinged again.

"Actually, I am. You?"

"Yeah. I'm working and I better get back to it. Catch ya later?" I peeked around the corner and watched her type away on her phone.

"Catch ya later, Mobile Man. Don't work too hard."

She set her phone down and took a seat at the table. I couldn't believe this. Eloise was Digits. Placing my phone back in my pocket, I took my seat and stared at her.

"What?" She smiled.

"Nothing. I'm just excited to see your work."

#*Delete*

"Okay. Go sit on the couch and I'll grab my portfolio. I can clean this up later."

I took a seat on the couch, and a few moments later, Eloise sat down next to me and opened her portfolio.

"Wow. These are really good," I spoke as I studied each page and photograph.

"Thank you."

"You definitely have a natural talent, and the kind of talent I need for the Chanel shoot."

"Would you like to see the wedding photos I took at the wedding we were both at?"

I looked over at her and could see the excitement in her eyes.

"Of course I would." I grinned.

She grabbed her laptop from the coffee table. Pulling up the file, she opened it and an array of pictures filled the screen.

"These are stunning, Eloise. What did the happy couple have to say?"

"They haven't seen them yet, so don't let on that you did."

I chuckled. "I won't. It'll be our little secret." I winked.

The thought that she was Digits harbored inside me. I wanted to reach out, place my hand on her beautiful cheek, and tell her that I was Mobile Man. But I couldn't. Not yet. It would more than likely freak her out and I couldn't have that.

"I should get going. It's getting late," I spoke.

"Yeah, okay."

We both got up from the couch and I started to help her clean up from dinner.

"You don't have to do that, Christian. I got this." She grinned.

"I want to help," I spoke as I grabbed the empty beer bottles from the table.

Once we finished cleaning up, she walked me to the door.

"By the way, did I mention that the photo shoot is in Chicago and we leave Friday morning?"

She cocked her head and raised her brow at me.

"No, you did not mention that."

"I hope it's not going to be a problem. We'll be back on Sunday."

"You're lucky I don't have any photo shoots this weekend." She smirked.

"I guess I am." I smirked back at her.

It took every bit of strength I had in me not to lean in and kiss her. The thought of her soft lips tangled with mine again excited me. I placed my hands in my pockets to stop any involuntary movement.

"Good night, Eloise. Oh, by the way, I know you don't want to give me your phone number, so just give me your email address and we can communicate through that."

"Well, since I'm doing a freelance job for you, it would only be professional of me to give you my number. Hold on a second and I'll go grab a piece of paper and a pen."

#Delete

A few moments later, she returned and handed me the small pink post-it note with her phone number on it.

"Thanks." I smiled. "Have a good night."

"You too, Christian." The corners of her mouth slightly curved upwards as she closed the door.

Chapter Nineteen

Eloise

As much as I tried to not focus on how intense the evening was with Christian, I couldn't help it. There was a part of me that had hoped his lips would have brushed mine. He was a perfect gentleman and didn't even try to come close to flirting with me. He was successful, nice, and sexy as hell. He seemed to be everything I wanted in a man. Well, I couldn't really say that, could I? I barely knew him. They all seemed that way at first, and once you invested time and energy in them and became attached, they pulled some shit that made you wish you never would have gotten involved in the first place. I turned off the lights in the living area and retreated to my bedroom for the night with my laptop.

I signed in to my blog and began writing a post regarding an email I received from a woman named Lina.

Dear Eloise,

I met this man four months ago and I fell head over heels for him right from the start. We connected instantly and have amazing and deep conversations. He's the same age as I am and has been married and divorced twice. I was hesitant to give him my number at first because I felt I wasn't ready to date, even though I'd been divorced two years. We started out emailing each other and then I felt comfortable enough to give him my number. He texted me instantly and we sent messages back and forth every day. In the four months we knew each other, we only went out on a date a couple of times and it was during the day. It seemed as though he was always busy, even when he didn't have his kids. Then one day, the texting stopped. I would text him and get a very short response. Either an emoji or a one-word sentence. He kept telling me over and over how much he really liked me but wasn't ready to jump into an official relationship. It's been over two weeks and I haven't heard a single word from him. I do have him as a Facebook friend and I can see he's online all the time, especially late at night. I don't know what to do. I really like him and I thought he liked me too. I'm having a hard time trying to forget him and the feeling of being rejected is killing me. Any advice would be greatly appreciated.

I felt for her and I could relate to everything she was feeling and going through with this douchebag. Just as I was about to write my blog post, my phone dinged with a text message from Mobile Man. Instantly, a smile crossed my lips.

"Hi there, beautiful. How's your evening?"

"Hi! Why are you calling me 'beautiful'? You have no clue what I look like. My evening is good. Just doing some work now."

"I don't have to know what you look like to think you're beautiful. That's the beauty of our text relationship. We can tell how the other person is just by our conversations."

"Is that so? Then what else am I?"

"I think you're a kind and sweet woman who is strong and independent. You know what you want and you'll stop at nothing to go after it."

"True, lol. Are you drunk?"

"Lol. No, I'm not drunk. I'm complimenting you. Isn't that what friends do?"

"I guess so. You seem different tonight. What's going on?"

"I took your advice about chasing the girl."

"Oh? And?"

"I made progress with her and I'm feeling really good."

"That's great, Mobile Man. I'm so happy for you!"

"Thanks, Digits. I couldn't have done it without you."

"Did you ask her out?"

"Not yet, but the time is coming. I'm taking it slow for now. I don't want to scare her off."

"I don't think you'll scare her off, but if you don't get anywhere with her in a couple of weeks' time, you may have to #Delete her. Or if she starts to display the whole bench, ghost, or breadcrumbing behavior."

"I don't think she'd do that."

"Nobody thinks the other person they're interested in would do that, but they do. Shit, Mobile Man, you've done it. It's too easy nowadays to avoid confrontation. Just be on the lookout. I don't want you to get hurt."

"You don't? Tell me why."

"Because you're my friend and all I want is for you to be happy."

"You don't even really know me, Digits."

"Call it my woman's intuition."

"If we're being honest, all I want is for you to be happy too. I want you to find the man of your dreams. A man who would never do those things to you and would never hurt you."

"Wow. That's deep. Thank you. I appreciate it, Mobile Man. But I'm not looking for the man of my dreams. I don't believe he exists."

"He does, Digits. I'm sure of it. Enjoy the rest of your evening. Catch ya later?"

"You too. Catch ya later."

I smiled as I set my phone down. The things Mobile Man said to me were sweet and it made me feel warm inside. Was he trying to make me fall for him? *Shit*. My emotions were running at an all-time high, between him and Christian.

Chapter Twenty

Christian

I was up all fucking night thinking about Digits, AKA Eloise. The dates she'd been on but the fact that she wouldn't go out with me burned a hole in my soul. How was I going to tell her that the man she'd been texting all this time was me? The most important question was when was I going to tell her? This was one secret I had to keep a little while longer, at least until after our Chicago trip. I was going to do everything I could to make that trip one she'd never forget.

As I was standing in line at Starbucks, grabbing a coffee before heading to the office, I pulled my phone from my pocket and sent a text message to Digits.

"Good morning. I hope you slept well."

"Good morning. I did. How about you?"

"Not bad," I lied. *"I hope you have a great day."*

"Thanks, Mobile Man. I hope you have a great day too."

"I will, Digits. Trust me! Catch ya later."

"Catch ya later."

With a smile on my face, I placed my phone back into my

#Delete

pocket, grabbed my coffee, and walked the two blocks to the office. Knowing that I was talking to Eloise made my day even brighter.

"Someone's in a fantastic mood." Claire smiled as I walked past her desk.

"Good morning, Claire. I am in a fantastic mood."

She got up from her chair and followed me into my office.

"Umm. How did things go with Eloise?"

"Things went well. Her portfolio is outstanding and the two of us leave for Chicago Friday morning."

"Good. I'm happy she accepted the job. So it's just going to be the two of you in Chicago for a couple of days?"

"Yes. Why? Well, the two of us and some of the people from Chanel."

"Just wondering. I didn't know if Peter or Jimmy were going."

"Nah. I need them here at the firm. Is there anything else?"

"No." She shook her head. "I'm going to get back to work." She slowly walked out of my office.

"Thanks, Claire."

****

Eloise

I was just heading out the door to deliver the wedding proofs to Kim and Grant when my phone rang.

"Hey, Claire, what's up?" I asked as I stepped out of my apartment building and onto the street.

"Did anything happen between you and Christian last night?"

"No." I laughed. Why?"

"He came in this morning in a really good mood. I thought maybe he spent the night."

"No, he didn't. We had pizza and beer, talked, I showed him my portfolio, and he left. He didn't try a thing. It was strictly professional."

"Oh, okay. Maybe he went out last night after he left your place."

"I don't know. Maybe."

After we said our goodbyes, a stinging sensation shot through my heart. The thought of Christian going out last night after leaving my place bothered me a bit. Maybe that was why he didn't try to kiss me? Or flirt with me? Maybe he was already going on a date and that was why he left when he did. Either way, I needed to stop thinking about it and him.

After dropping off the proofs, I headed to Starbucks for a cup of coffee on my way home. I was waiting in line for my drink to be made when I overheard two women complaining about men. My ears perked up instantly.

"Iced Grande caramel macchiato with nonfat milk for Eloise," the barista spoke.

"Thank you." I smiled.

After grabbing my coffee from the counter, I walked over to

#Delete

the table where the two women sat. They were both in their late twenties, early thirties at the most.

"Excuse me," I spoke. "I couldn't help overhear about your man issues."

Both women glared at me like I had some nerve intruding on their private conversation.

"I'm sorry. I'm Eloise." I held out my hand. "I have a dating blog. *The Chronicles of #Delete*."

"I'm Sara and this is my friend, Tia."

"Nice to meet you both," I spoke.

"Please have a seat." Sara gestured.

"You say you have a dating blog?" Tia asked.

"Yes. My goal is to teach women about the concept of #Delete before they get too involved with a man. To help them see the red flags that pop up in the early stages of dating."

"Well, there's this man I met a couple of months ago," Sara began to speak. "We hit it off instantly and exchanged numbers. That same night, we talked on the phone for over two hours. After that, I didn't hear from him for three days. So, I reached out to him and we set up a date. He took me to dinner and then we walked in Central Park and talked about life. After our date, he told me he'd call me the next day. A week went by and he never called or texted me. I spent that week replaying our date in my head, trying to see what could have gone wrong. Then, another week went by, and just when I was putting him out of my mind, he sent me a text message and asked how I was doing."

"Let me guess." I smiled. "You instantly replied."

"I did. I was just so happy that I finally heard from him."

"What did you respond with?" I asked.

"I told him that I was doing good and how happy I was to hear from him. He said he'd been thinking about me and he was sorry he hadn't been in touch, but he was working crazy hours because he's up for a promotion. He also said that he'd be in touch in a couple of days when he had a better handle on his schedule and he'd take me out."

"Did he get in touch with you?" I arched my brow because I already knew the answer.

"He did. Exactly nine days later. Once again asking me how I was and if I missed him."

I placed my hand over my face and slowly shook my head.

"Please tell me you didn't tell him you did."

"Yep. She told him," Tia spoke.

"Did he end up taking you out?" I asked.

"No." Sara looked down in embarrassment. "It's become a pattern with him. He'll text me every other week and hand me some excuse as to why he hadn't been in touch."

"Wait, it gets better." Tia smiled.

I looked at Sara with a narrowed eye. "What happened?"

"I joined a new gym and ran into him there last week. I could tell by the look on his face that he was shocked to see me. I asked him how he was doing. He told me his hard work paid off and he got the promotion and that he'd have some free time now to go out. We made small talk and he left."

"Have you heard from him since the gym meeting?"

"No, and I can't stop thinking about him. I hate this, and I don't know what to do."

"I'll tell you what you're going to do," I spoke. "You're going to delete his number from your phone and pretend he never existed."

"I don't think I can. I just feel in my heart there's a possibility he's going to take me out."

"Listen, Sara." I reached across the table and placed my hand on hers. "What he's doing is a term called breadcrumbing."

"What?" Her brows furrowed.

"It's when a guy will reach out to you when he's feeling bored or lonely. It's an ego boost for him knowing you're still out there hanging on. He's throwing you little breadcrumbs to keep you interested without any intention of taking you out or getting serious. I can guarantee he has a lot of women in his life that he's doing this to."

"But we already went on a date," she spoke. "That's what I don't understand."

"Maybe he wasn't feeling it, or maybe he knew if he took you out at least once, that would be enough to get you hooked."

"But I miss him." She pouted.

"Let me ask you this. What is it that you miss about him? Are you really attached to him or to the outcome of this relationship? Because sometimes, we women aren't really into the guy as much as we think we are."

I reached into my purse and took out a pen and my small notepad. Drawing a line down the center of the paper, I labeled the left side PROS, and the right side CONS. After placing it in front of her, I spoke, "I want you to list all the pros and cons of this guy."

She picked up the pen and began writing. Once she was finished, she looked at both sides. On the left side that was labeled PROS, she had written down three things about him. On the right side that was labeled CONS, the column consisted of eight things that she found wrong with him.

"Hmm," she spoke as she studied what she wrote down. "The cons outweigh the pros."

"Exactly." I smiled. "You are a beautiful woman with high standards and self-worth. This loser who only contacts you when it suits him is a waste of your time. And the longer you hold on to the hope that he'll call and ask you out again, the longer you are blocking your dream guy from walking into your life."

"Oh my God, Eloise, you're right. I don't deserve to be treated this way."

"No, you don't. This man is low investment. Women don't have time to put up with low-investment men. If he isn't high investment, it's time to #Delete."

"So what should I do if by chance he crawls out of the woodwork and texts me again?"

"You respond with this: 'Your time to talk to me has expired. Bye.' Then swipe and delete."

#Delete

"I love you!" She grinned as she threw her arms around me from across the table.

"You should really host some dating classes or make videos," Tia spoke. "You're very inspiring. I am totally going to follow your blog."

"Me too!" Sara smiled. "Thank you, Eloise. You have no idea how much you've helped me today."

"You're welcome." I got up from my seat. "Let me know what happens. You can find all my contact information on my blog."

Chapter Twenty-One

Eloise

I left Starbucks feeling like a million bucks. Knowing that I helped Sara realize the man she liked was a total douchebag and that she was wasting her time made me feel incredible. I was walking down the street, reveling in my glory, when I turned the corner and literally ran into Luke.

"Eloise," he spoke in shock as he lightly touched my arm.

It was inevitable that we'd eventually run into each other. Even though there are eight million people who live in New York City, it would be my luck to run into the douchebags who quickly entered and then just as quickly exited my life.

"Sorry. I didn't see you," I spoke as I tried to walk past him.

"Wait. You look great. How are you?"

I gave him a cunning smile.

"I'm fantastic!"

He looked like he hadn't shaven in days and his hair was in bad need of a cut.

"Listen, I know you said some things to me during our last conversation, but I was wondering if maybe you wanted to go

#Delete

get a drink? I don't have the kids tonight."

There was a laughter inside me that was dying to escape. But instead, I stood there smiling at him.

"Let me ask you a question. Can you see the 'Fuck you' in my smile?"

He stood there, staring at me with a narrowed eye.

"Fine. I guess that's a no. Have a good life, Eloise. I won't bother you again."

"Thank you, Luke. I really do hope you get your life together. Just do me one favor."

"What's that?" he asked.

"Don't toy with women's emotions. If you don't want to date anyone right now, just stay away from women altogether. Don't lead them on and make them think they're special. And for the love of God, just be honest from the beginning. It'll save you a lot of trouble." I began to walk away.

"One more thing, Eloise."

I stopped, rolled my eyes, and turned around.

"I am sorry."

I gave him a small smile and headed home. Just as I opened the door to my apartment, my phone dinged. Pulling it from my purse, I saw I had a text message from Mobile Man.

"How's your day going?"

"It's fabulous!"

"That's what I like to hear. Anything special happen to put

you in such a fabulous mood?"

"As a matter of fact, I helped a woman out at Starbucks with a relationship issue."

"Ah. Good for you. So, I guess you're an expert."

"Lol. Not yet, but I'm on my way. In fact, I have to go get ready for a singles mixer I'm attending tonight."

"Oh. You're going to one of those?"

"Yes. Catch ya later?"

"Sure. Catch ya later."

****

Christian

I threw my phone across my desk and leaned back in my chair. The fucking thought of her going to a single's mixer and potentially meeting someone enraged me. Jealousy coursed through my body the more I thought about it.

"Fuck!" I yelled.

"Are you okay, Christian?" Claire asked as she stepped into my office.

"NO!"

I stood up from my seat and tucked my hands in my pockets as I paced around the room.

"Anything I can do to help?"

"Yeah. You can stop your friend from going to a singles mixer tonight," I accidentally blurted out.

#Delete

"What? Who? You mean Eloise?"

Shit. Shit. Shit.

"I shouldn't have said that. I'm sorry," I spoke. "Just forget it."

"She told you she's going to a single's mixer tonight?"

I heavily sighed as I ran my hand through my hair.

"Why would she tell you that?" she asked.

"She didn't tell me that."

"Then how do you know?" she asked in confusion.

I sat down in my chair and placed my face in my hands. How the fuck was I going to get out of this one?

"Christian, what the hell is going on? If Eloise didn't tell you she's going, then how did you find out? Are you stalking her or something? Having her followed? Tapping her phone."

"Don't be ridiculous, Claire. Do you honestly think I would do any of those things?"

"None of this makes sense."

I inhaled a deep breath.

"Eloise didn't tell me directly; Digits did," I spoke as I stared at her.

Fuck. I had no choice.

Her brows furrowed and the look on her face told me she was in a state of confusion. She was one of Eloise's best friends, and I was sure she told her about Mobile Man.

"Wait a minute." She put her hand up. "How do you know about Digits?"

I grabbed my phone from my desk, brought up our text messages, and showed it to Claire. After a moment, she placed her hand over her mouth and looked at me with wide eyes.

"You're Mobile Man?"

"Yes."

"Holy shit. Does Eloise know?"

"No, and you are not to tell her either. Do you understand me? I just found out when I went to her apartment to look at her portfolio. I asked her about her parents and she told me word for word what Digits told me in our text messages."

"I have no words right now, Christian. Absolutely no words."

"I'm still in shock myself."

"You have to tell her."

"I will. Just not right now. I'm planning on it after the Chicago trip."

"Why? Why are you waiting?" she asked.

"Because I want to make Chicago a trip she'll never forget, Claire. If I tell her that I'm Mobile Man, she may never talk to me again."

"But you don't know that for sure. She likes Mobile Man a lot. Like, every time I'm with her and a text from you comes through, she gets this big smile on her face. She already feels the connection, so her knowing won't change that."

#Delete

"It's a chance I'm not willing to take yet. Please, don't tell her."

She sat there in the chair shaking her head as her eyes burned into mine.

"I won't. I want nothing to do with this. If she ever found out I knew, she would probably end our friendship."

"Then forget about it. This conversation never happened."

"You're right." She got up from her seat. "It never happened. As for her going to the singles mixer tonight, you have nothing to worry about. She's not out to find a man. She's only using them for their dumb brains. No offense."

"No offense taken." I smiled.

Chapter Twenty-Two

Eloise

I spent the rest of the day cleaning my apartment and getting it ready so I could film a video for my blog. Ghosting had seemed to be a huge issue with guys, so I wanted to tackle that topic first. As I was setting up my camera, my phone dinged. When I looked at the number, it was one I'd never seen before. Opening my text messages, I saw it was from Christian. My belly did a flip and I quietly told it to stop.

"Hi, Eloise, it's Christian. I just wanted to send you a quick text to let you know that our flight for Chicago leaves Friday morning at seven a.m. I'll swing by and pick you up around five a.m."

"Hi, Christian. Sounds good. I'll be ready."

"In the meantime, if you have any questions, feel free to call me."

"Thank you. I will."

Five a.m.? Ugh. I'd have to make sure everything was packed and sitting by the door the night before. Setting my phone down, I lit the candles I had sitting on the table and took a seat on my white leather couch. Turning my camera on, I began to film my video. Once I finished, it was time to get

#Delete

ready for the singles mixer I was attending tonight.

****

Christian

I turned off my computer, grabbed my briefcase, and as I was walking out of my office for the evening, Claire stopped me.

"Christian?"

"What's up, Claire? I'm leaving for the day."

She handed me a folded white piece of paper and walked away.

Singles Mixer

Empire Hotel Rooftop Lounge

7:30 p.m.

After reading the note, I looked up and Claire was already gone. Folding the paper and placing it in my pocket, I headed down to Peter's office.

"Hey." I lightly tapped on the door before stepping inside.

"Hey. You're leaving already?" he asked.

"Yeah. What are you doing tonight?"

"Actually, I was going to ask you the same thing. I was thinking some drinking at the bar was in order."

"I've got something better."

"What?"

"A singles mixer at the Empire Hotel Rooftop Lounge at 7:30."

He laughed. "Since when do you go to a singles mixer?"

"I don't. I've never needed to, but someone is going to be there tonight."

"Who?" He cocked his head.

"Eloise."

"She won't go out with you, but she'll go to a singles mixer?" He laughed.

"I guess so. Are you up for going? Maybe you'll meet the woman of your dreams there."

"Why not." He shrugged. "I'm going to stay back and finish up the Levitt's Campaign. I'll meet you there."

"Sounds good."

****

Eloise

As I was in the bathroom getting ready to go out, I heard a knock at my door. I set down my makeup brush, walked over, and looked through the peephole only to find Claire standing there.

"Hi." I smiled as I opened the door. "What are you doing here?"

"I've decided to go to the singles mixer with you."

"Are you serious? Come on in. I'm almost ready. Isn't Kenny going to be pissed you're going?"

#Delete

"Kenny doesn't know. He's out with the guys playing cards. I told him me and you were going to dinner and then hanging at your place after."

"I'm not thrilled that you lied to him, but I'm happy you're coming along with me."

"Meh." She shrugged. "He tells me little white lies all the time."

I put the finishing touches on my makeup, lightly sprayed my hair, and we headed to the Empire Hotel. When we arrived, we were escorted to the Rooftop Lounge where single men and women from New York City gathered. It was a beautiful fall night and the ambiance was perfect. Over towards the corner of the rooftop, we found an empty couch, so we ran to it as fast as we could and took a seat.

"Wow. This is great. I've never been to one of these before." Claire smiled.

"Me either. It's pretty cool."

Men walked past us, smiling, winking, giving us the "I may want to fuck you" look. They swarmed around us like eagles searching for their prey.

"Hi there. I'm Jack." The cute guy who stood approximately five foot eight smiled.

"Hello." I smiled back. "I'm Eloise."

"What an unusual and beautiful name."

"Thanks, I think. This is my friend, Claire, but she's not single. She's just tagging along."

"Friend support, I like that. Would you mind if I took a

seat?"

"No. Not at all." I patted the spot next to me.

"I see you ladies don't have drinks yet. May I get you something from the bar?"

"I'll have a cosmopolitan." I casually smiled.

"And I'll have a glass of Pinot," Claire spoke.

After Jack left to go to the bar, Claire excused herself to the bathroom. I sat there, watching all the men and women mingle, wondering how many of them would find someone tonight and how many of the men wouldn't call the next day. While I waited for my drink and Claire, I pulled out my phone and sent a message to Mobile Man.

"Hi. I'm on the hunt, lol."

"Hi. Just be careful. There are some real weirdos out there. If you need me, text me." He sent the winky face.

"Thanks. But I can take care of myself."

I looked up from my phone and gasped when I saw Christian and his friend Peter walk in. My heart started racing and the air around me became thick.

"Here you go." Jack smiled as he handed me my drink. "Where's your friend?"

"Right behind you," Claire replied.

"Excuse us for a moment, Jack, but I need to speak with Claire."

Grabbing hold of her arm, I led her over in the opposite

corner behind a plastic palm tree.

"What?" she asked.

"Why the fuck is Christian here?" I spoke through gritted teeth.

"Huh? Oh my God!" she shrieked. "Christian is here? Where?" She looked around.

"Over there!" I pointed. "By the bar."

Her eyes diverted over to the bar. "He's with Peter."

"Yeah. I can see that. We have to get out of here!" I exclaimed.

"Why?"

"Because what will he think? I turned down his offer to take me out and now I'm at a singles mixer?"

"Oh yeah. I forgot about that. Not to mention you had sex with him."

"Ugh! Let's go."

I downed my drink as fast as I could.

"How are we going to sneak out?" Claire asked. "He's going to see us."

"Follow me."

I grabbed her hand, ducked down, and tried to weave in and out of the crowd of people.

Chapter Twenty-Three

Christian

The moment I walked in, I spotted Eloise sitting on the couch looking down at her phone. I needed to act casual, so Peter and I hit the bar first for a drink. While we were waiting for our drinks to be made, I saw Eloise and Claire trying to escape. She must have seen me, but I wasn't going to let her get away that easily.

"Peter, stop those two." I pointed. "I'll grab our drinks. Be casual."

Peter smiled and headed toward Eloise and Claire while I stood there and watched him stop them dead in their tracks. After grabbing our drinks from the bar, I walked over to where the three of them were standing.

"Eloise? Claire? What are you doing here?" I asked as I handed Peter his drink.

"Why wouldn't we be here? It's a singles mixer," Claire spoke.

"But you're not single."

"She's here with me," Eloise spoke as she stood tall. "What are *you* doing here?"

#Delete

"Like she said, it's a singles mixer and I'm single." I smirked.

"You don't appear to be the type to come to these things," she spoke.

"What type does a person have to be to attend?" I arched my brow."

"Well, I'm here taking photographs for an article."

"Where's your camera?" I asked with a narrowed eye.

Peter took Claire by the arm and escorted her to the bar to give Eloise and me some alone time.

"I'm taking pictures with my phone. Smile," she spoke as she snapped a picture of me.

"I think you're lying. You wouldn't do that."

"Fine, Christian. It's a long story and I really don't want to get into it."

"I have all night, sweetheart." I grinned.

"I'm doing research for a blog I run. It's for relationship advice."

I chuckled.

"You, the woman who won't go out on a date with me, gives relationship advice?"

"It's complicated."

"So you're not here to meet anyone special?" I asked.

"No. It's purely business/blog related. I told you that I'm not ready to date anyone. I swear I'm telling you the truth."

"Okay. Well, I am here to explore my options, so I'll let you go do your research."

"You are?" She cocked her head.

"Of course. Why else would I be here?" I smiled.

Peter and Claire walked over to us and I held my glass up to Peter's.

"Let's go explore our options. Shall we?" I grinned.

"We shall." Peter smiled as he tipped his glass against mine.

****

Eloise

Christian and Peter walked away and I stood there with a feeling of—I don't know what the hell it was. All I knew was that I was uncomfortable with Christian being here.

"See." Claire smiled. "No big deal. You were worried for nothing."

I swallowed hard as I watched Christian walk up to some tall brunette who had more Botox and fillers than natural beauty.

"Whatever." I scowled at her and walked away.

"There you are, Eloise." Jack smiled. "Can we get to know each other better now?"

I glanced over at Christian, who was laughing with the brunette and lightly touching her arm.

"Of course we can." I hooked my arm around Jack's.

#Delete

I led him over by the bar and he ordered me another cosmopolitan. After he handed me my drink, we took a seat on an empty couch and began to talk. My eyes wouldn't stop diverting over to where Christian was flirting with that woman. A lump grew in the back of my throat with each finger stroke down her arm and her finger strokes down his chest.

"Eloise? Am I boring you or something?" Jack asked.

"Umm. No, of course not. I have some questions for you if you don't mind."

"Go ahead and ask away." He smiled.

I questioned him, and he willingly answered but with a strange look on his face.

"These are some really weird questions. Maybe you're not the woman I thought you were." He got up from the couch.

"In all honesty, Jack, I'm not." I lightly smiled.

"Well then, I'll be moving on."

I gave him a nod just as Claire walked over and sat down.

"Where were you?" I asked.

"Checking out the crowd, being hit on, and listening in on people's conversations." She grinned.

I finished my drink just as Christian walked over to me and Claire.

"Any luck?" He smirked.

"Not really. But I see you found someone." I cocked my head.

"You mean Brio? She's a nice woman and she wants to go out with me."

"Good for you, Christian." I stood up and patted his chest. "I hope the two of you have fun."

There was a discontent, an anger, so to speak, rising in my chest. I needed to get out of here and fast.

"Are you ready, Claire?"

"Yeah. If you are."

"I'm more than ready." I looked at Christian. "Enjoy the rest of your evening, Mr. Blake. I'll see you in a couple of days."

"You too, Miss Moore," he spoke with a cocky attitude.

I grabbed Claire by the hand and high-tailed it off the rooftop as quickly as I could.

"What is wrong with you? You can't seriously be jealous about Christian. You turned him down, remember?" she spoke.

"I remember and I'm not jealous. I'm tired and I want to go home."

We climbed into the back of a cab and since Claire's apartment was closer, the driver dropped her off first.

"You know you can always change your mind about going out with Christian."

"I'm not changing my mind. I don't give a fuck who he dates. But it sure as hell isn't going to be me."

She sighed as she climbed out of the cab and shut the door. Pulling out my phone, I sent a text message to the only person who I knew would make me feel okay.

"Hey. Sort of a bad night."

"Hey. Your singles mixer didn't go too well?"

"Not really."

"Want to talk about it?"

"It's just this guy that wants me to go out with him. He was there and he ended up meeting someone."

"Ah. Why won't you go out with this guy? You're always going on dates."

"Because he's the type of man I could fall for in a second, and that's something I don't want."

"All because of your past relationships?"

"Yeah. I guess. I'm taking a break from guys and serious dating."

"What's the harm, Digits? Maybe the two of you won't even hit it off and then you don't have to worry about it."

"Trust me, we'll hit it off. The physical attraction is so strong. I have to tell you something."

"What is it?"

"We had sex in his bathroom not too long ago. It just happened and I freaked out. Now I'm going to be doing a freelance job for him. We're going to Chicago on Friday."

"So after you had sex and freaked out, you still talk to him?"

"Sort of. I ran into him the next day and he apologized to me *for the bathroom sex."*

"That was nice of him. I would say he was a true gentleman to do that."

"He is. He's a great guy."

"Then what's the problem"

"The problem is I can't give myself to anyone again. At least not for a long time. I have other things I need to focus on and guys and dating aren't one of them. I need to focus solely on myself for now."

"You never know, Digits. He could be the one to change your life."

"Or he could be the one to destroy it."

"You're being paranoid."

"I have reason to be, Mobile Man."

"Some of the greatest gifts in life are on the other side of fear. I think you're afraid to get hurt again, so you've put up this wall around your heart."

"He's a serial dater and he never commits. For once in my life, I'm using my head. I just got home and I'm exhausted. Catch ya later?"

"Catch ya later, Digits. Good night."

"Good night, Mobile Man."

#Delete

Chapter Twenty-Four

Christian

I set my phone down and sighed. She was definitely jealous about Brio, and in a weird way, that made me happy. She did like me, and I knew damn well she was interested, but she was resisting. Hopefully, after our trip to Chicago, she would feel differently.

Picking up my phone, I sent a text message to Claire.

"Hi, Claire. Thank you for tonight."

"You're welcome, Christian, but I hated doing that to my best friend. If I didn't think you were the right guy for her, I wouldn't have done it."

"I know you wouldn't have and I appreciate it. I'll see you tomorrow at the office."

"See you tomorrow."

The next morning, I stopped at Starbucks to grab a cup of coffee before heading into the office. As I stepped inside, I turned around to see if anyone was behind me to hold the door open. That was when I saw Eloise walk up.

"Good morning." I smiled.

"Christian. Good morning," she spoke as she looked at me with confusion. "What are you doing here? Don't you have coffee at your office?" She smirked.

"I do, but sometimes I like to stop here and grab a cup on the way. What about you? Don't you have a coffee maker at home?"

"I do, but I like what Starbucks has to offer better."

"Actually, I'm glad I ran into you. Since we're leaving tomorrow morning for Chicago, I thought maybe sometime today or tonight, we could sit down and go over a few ideas for the shoot."

"I was wondering about that. I thought maybe you just trusted me enough to wing it." She grinned.

"I do, but I think it's in both our best interest to have a meeting first. Just so neither one of us catches the other off guard."

"I agree. I'm sure dinner is out of the question since you're probably going out with that woman from last night."

"Actually, I haven't set anything up with her yet, so I am free tonight. That is, if you're free. Or are you planning on attending another singles mixer?"

She let out a light laugh, which made my smile grow wide.

"I think I'm done with those singles mixers."

"Then how about dinner? Strictly professional." I put up my hands. "All we'll talk about is business."

She glared at me for a moment and then the woman that was standing behind her spoke up.

#Delete

"You'd be crazy not to have dinner with him. Even if it is strictly business." She winked.

Eloise turned and looked at me.

"Dinner will be fine, but I can't be out late since our flight leaves at an ungodly hour in the morning."

"I agree. I can pick you up around six o'clock."

"Just tell me which restaurant and I'll meet you there at six." She smirked.

"Shit, honey, I'd give anything for him to come to my house and pick me up," the woman behind her spoke.

I gave the woman a small smile and then it was my turn to order.

"Your coffee is on me today, Eloise. Tell her what you want. And you also, miss." I smiled.

As soon as our coffee was ready, the woman thanked me and began fanning herself while she looked at Eloise as she walked out of Starbucks.

"That was nice of you to buy her coffee. You made her day," Eloise spoke.

"It's the least I could do since she was rooting for me." I smirked.

"How about Tavern on the Green tonight?" she asked as we both walked out the door.

"Sounds good. I'll see you at six." I winked as I walked down the street and hailed a cab.

What a way to start off the day. I could spend every morning seeing her first thing before heading into the office. She looked as beautiful as ever, and not only was I looking forward to our dinner tonight, I couldn't wait to spend the next three days with her in Chicago.

When I arrived at the office, my phone dinged with a text message from Digits. A smile crossed my lips.

"Good morning, sunshine!"

"Good morning. You seem to be in a good mood. Feeling better from last night?"

"I am. I wanted to thank you for listening to me last night. I know I kind of dumped a lot on you."

"You're welcome. That's what friends are for. Plus, I like being here for you."

"Thanks. I'm here for you too, Mobile Man. Don't ever forget that."

"I won't. I appreciate you, Digits."

"I appreciate you too. Any progress on the woman situation?"

"A little bit." I sent the smiley emoji.

"Good to hear. I just got home and need to start doing some work now. Catch ya later?"

"Always. Catch ya later, Digits. Have a great day."

"You too, Mobile Man."

"I already am."

#*Delete*

After an awesome productivity meeting with my staff, Peter followed me back to my office.

"Guess who has a date tonight?" he spoke.

"I'm going to go out on a limb here and say you do."

"That's right." He smirked. "I texted Rebecca this morning and we're having dinner tonight."

"Is she the blonde you were talking to at the singles mixer?"

"She sure is." He grinned.

"Good for you, Peter. I'm having dinner tonight with Eloise. We're going to go over some ideas for the Chanel shoot."

"Looks like we're both scoring tonight." He fist-bumped me.

"My dinner is strictly business."

"How are things going with that chick you text every day? Any chance of meeting her yet?"

"Nah. She likes things the way they are and I respect that."

"I still think she's probably some two-hundred-fifty-pound girl who sits on the couch with a computer in her lap all day. Why else wouldn't she want to meet you? She's probably embarrassed by the way she looks."

"Looks aren't everything. She's a nice girl and I like talking to her."

"Suit yourself, bro. I still think it's fucking weird, and looks aren't everything? Yeah, right." He laughed.

"Don't you have work to do?" I asked with annoyance.

"Yeah. I'll see you later."

#Delete

Chapter Twenty-Five

Eloise

When I arrived back home, I set my coffee cup down on the table, grabbed my laptop, and began editing yesterday's blog video. I was almost finished with the last edit when my phone rang. I looked over and saw it was Natalie face-timing me.

"Hello," I answered with a smile.

"Hello, darling. What is this I hear about you going to Chicago with Christian Blake? And why haven't you told me?" she asked with a hint of irritation.

"I've been busy with work. I'm sorry. It kind of happened so fast. I'm doing a Chanel photo shoot for Christian's advertising agency. Isn't that exciting?"

"Chanel is exciting, yes. But, my lovely grounded friend, I'm not so sure going with Christian is a good idea. You may get swept up in the windy city with him. Which, of course, is fine if that's what you want."

I rolled my eyes at her.

"This trip is strictly business. Besides, he met someone at the singles mixer last night. Her name is Brio. Like, seriously, what kind of name is that?" I frowned.

"I sense a hint of jealousy in your tone." She smiled.

"Ha. I'm not jealous at all. It's just her name is weird. Don't you think?"

She shrugged. "I think it's kind of cool and different."

"Whatever. Anyway, I'm almost finished with the edits for my first blog video. As soon as I'm done, I'll send it over to you."

"Sounds good. I can't wait to see it. By the way, are you still talking to that Mobile Man guy?"

"Yes. Every day." I grinned. "I'm actually giving him some advice on a woman he's interested in."

"So he texts you every day? And responds in a timely manner?"

"Yes. He usually responds right away and vice versa."

"Sounds like the perfect man to me. I think you should meet him."

"I think not." I arched my brow. "Enough about him. How's Hawaii and Nathan?"

"Hawaii is amazing and so is Nathan. Unfortunately, he had to fly back to Long Island today. But he said as soon as I get back, he's taking me out."

"You slept with him, didn't you?" I asked.

"Maybe." She smiled.

"Well, I'm happy for you."

"Thanks, doll. I could be happy for you too if you let your

#Delete

guard down and meet Mobile Man. He sounds like a nice guy."

"He is and we're text buddies and that's all we'll ever be."

She sighed and rolled her eyes.

"I have to go. I'll be home in a few days and we'll catch up."

"Okay. Enjoy the rest of your trip."

"Enjoy Chicago, and if anything happens, you better call me right away! I don't want to be hearing about it from Claire or Scarlett."

"I will." I laughed.

I finished the edits and sent the video off to Natalie, Claire, and Scarlett, then proceeded to upload it to my blog. I also decided to start a YouTube channel. What better way to reach millions of women from all over the world.

After I finished recording my second video, it was time for me to freshen up and get ready for dinner with Christian. I hated the fact that a bit of excitement fluttered inside me. I was putting my shoes on when I heard my phone ding.

"Plans tonight?" Mobile Man asked.

"Actually, yes. I'm just heading out to dinner."

"A date?"

"No. It's a business dinner. You?"

"Having dinner with a beautiful woman."

"I hope you mean the same woman you're chasing after."

"Of course. She's the only woman I'm interested in."

"Good for you! How did you get her to have dinner with you?"

"I took your advice. So once again, thank you."

"You're welcome. I hope it goes well for you. Don't be a douchebag."

"I promise I won't be. In fact, I don't think I ever could be with this woman."

"Sounds like you might have found your soulmate, Mobile Man."

"Maybe I have, Digits. We'll see. Enjoy your business dinner. Catch ya later?"

"Always. I want all the details. Catch ya later."

****

I stepped inside Tavern on the Green and told the hostess I was meeting someone.

"Hi, I'm meeting Christian Blake. Is he here yet?"

"He is." She nodded. "Follow me."

I followed her to a table that sat in the middle of the restaurant and took the seat across from Christian.

"Hi." He smiled.

"Hi."

"I've taken the liberty of ordering a bottle of their house wine. I hope that's okay."

"Sounds good. Thank you." I placed my napkin in my lap.

#Delete

Swan dives were happening in the pit of my stomach as I looked at him. This feeling was torturous and I needed it to stop.

"Are you all packed for Chicago?" he asked as we both glanced over the menu.

"No." I lightly laughed. "I'll do that when I get home. Are you?"

"No." He smirked. "If you have a formal dress, it would be wise to bring it. We will be attending a Chanel dinner on Friday night."

"Do you always do this?" I cocked my head.

"Do what?"

"Wait until the last minute to spring stuff on people?"

He chuckled. "I'm sorry. I just found out about the dinner right before I arrived at the restaurant."

"Oh. Well, in that case, you're forgiven. And I do have a formal dress I can bring."

"Good. I'm sure it looks beautiful on you." He winked.

I could feel the rise of heat in my cheeks. After we placed our dinner order, Christian and I got down to business. As we were talking about the shoot and jotting down some ideas, a woman stopped at our table and glared at Christian.

"Well. Well. Look who it is. Mr. Christian Blake," the woman spoke in a harsh tone.

Christian cleared his throat. "Hello, Cheyenne."

"Is that all you can say?" she asked with her hands placed

firmly on her hips. "I haven't heard from you since our date. I sent you a few text messages only to never get a response from you."

"I'm sorry. I've been really busy."

"Too busy to shoot a fucking text back? A text that would literally take thirty seconds or less of your time?"

"Now isn't the time, Cheyenne," Christian spoke in irritation.

"Who's this?" She looked over at me with an evil eye. "Is this your first date? 'Cause guess what, honey, he won't be calling you after tonight."

It was apparent Christian had ghosted her and she was angry. I didn't blame her because I'd been in her shoes more times than I could count.

"He isn't worth it, Cheyenne," I spoke.

"Excuse me?" She cocked her head.

"The anger, the resentment, the hurt. You're a beautiful woman. I can tell you're confident and you're strong. You know your self-worth, don't you?"

"Of course I do." She arched her brow.

"Then you know you're better than him and he doesn't deserve this attention you're giving right now. And you know why?"

"Why?" she asked.

"Because you're giving him power over you. And you don't strike me as the type of woman who would let someone have

#Delete

that kind of power. He clearly has communication issues and emotional immaturity if he couldn't extend the courtesy of texting you back. Is that the kind of man you want to be with or even go on a date with?"

"No." She shook her head.

"I didn't think so. Do you still have his number in your phone?"

"Yes. Why?"

"I want you to delete his number right now. You can do it, Cheyenne. Having his number in your phone is still giving him power over you. Because I know there's this little bit of hope that you'll still hear from him. Am I right?"

"Maybe."

"Take back your power." I smiled.

"You're right." She pulled out her phone, held it up to Christian, and deleted his number in front of him. "You're history, Mr. Blake." Cheyenne turned to me, and with a smile, she spoke, "I hope you'll take your own advice if he does the same to you."

"He won't. We aren't dating. I'm doing some photography work for his advertising agency. This is nothing but a business dinner. But if you should need any further assistance or advice on dating, here's my business card." I smiled as I handed it to her.

"Thank you." She grinned as she took it from me and walked away.

"Really?" I arched my brow at him.

"Really what?"

"You ghosted her?" I cocked my head.

He sighed and rolled his eyes.

"Yeah. I guess I did."

"And you think that's okay?"

"No. Not after hearing what you just said to her. And for the record, I am not emotionally immature." He pointed at me.

"You are if you did that. What is it with you guys and confrontation?"

"I didn't want to hurt her feelings by telling her I didn't want to see her again." He finished off his wine.

"And you don't think that going ghost is hurting her feelings?"

"I'm sorry. I didn't look at it that way. I just figured if I didn't text her back, she'd get the hint."

"Women need closure, Christian. Even if it was only after one date. It's called respect."

"Okay. I get it. I really do. But it's done now. So let's get back to discussing ideas for the shoot."

I folded my arms and sat up straight in my chair.

"You need to apologize to her."

Chapter Twenty-Six

Christian

Shit. I knew that was coming. She made me do it with Victoria, or should I say Digits did. I thought maybe I was off the hook when she didn't make me do it while Cheyenne was standing there. I glared at her from across the table, but I knew how important this was to her. Even though she never directly told me about what she was doing, I knew everything from what she as Digits told me via text.

"Fine. I will apologize to her," I spoke as I got up from my seat and walked over to where Cheyenne was sitting and waiting for someone to join her. "Excuse me, Cheyenne. May I have a word with you?"

"We're done speaking, Christian." Her brow arched at me.

"This will only take a minute. I want to apologize to you. I'm sorry for ignoring your text messages and not calling you after our date. It was rude and disrespectful and I had no idea that it would upset you. You didn't deserve that."

"You're right. I didn't deserve it, but since you were man enough to apologize, I accept."

"Thank you. I appreciate it."

"Now move along. My date will be here shortly," she spoke

as she sipped her drink.

Walking back to the table, I took my seat and stared at Eloise, who was sitting there with a grin on her face.

"Thank you." She held up her glass to me.

"No. Thank you." I smiled as I clinked my glass against hers.

After we finished dinner and talked some more about the Chanel shoot, I paid the bill and we left the restaurant.

"I think that was a very productive business dinner." I smiled.

"I think so too."

"You are actually on my way home. How about sharing a cab?"

"Sure." The corners of her mouth curved upwards.

I hailed us a cab and climbed in next to her. Since our dinner consisted mostly of business talk, I thought this would be a good opportunity to ask her about her blog, even though I already knew a little about it.

"When we were at the singles mixer, you mentioned something about your blog and about relationship advice. What exactly did you mean by that?" I asked.

"It's really no big deal." She waved her hand in front of her face.

"I'd still like to hear about it."

I could see the hesitation in her eyes as she stared at me for a moment.

#*Delete*

"I'm doing a piece on #Delete. It's for women who are in the early stages of a relationship."

"And what does that mean?" I asked.

"I want to empower women to know their self-worth and standards when dating a guy. So, if a guy behaves badly, it's in their best interest to delete them from their phone and life before they get too involved."

"And what qualifies as a man behaving badly?" I narrowed my eye at her.

"Ghosting would be number one." Her brow arched. "Low investment, lying, benching, breadcrumbing. The point is if a guy is really interested in a woman, he would do whatever it takes to get to know her. Texting in a timely manner, calling when he says he will, never flaking on a date. That would be considered high investment. If a guy is just stringing the girl along and has no intentions of wanting a relationship with her, then it's time for him to go."

"I see. And how does a girl know if the guy is just stringing her along."

"They never commit to dates. They send text messages sporadically when they're bored or lonely with the hopes that the woman is still waiting around, and when they get that reply, their ego gets boosted for a while and they're satisfied. Then they'll disappear again for a while and suddenly poof, send another text message. The problem is women become attached too quickly. They dive in with both feet and ignore the red flags that pop up."

"Is that something you've done or do?"

"I've done it many times in my life. And no, it's something

I don't anymore. I'm happy being single and I believe that's what women need to learn first. I'd spent too many years trying to find the perfect man like my dad because I wanted the kind of relationship he and my mom have. I guess you could say I was obsessed. And because of that, I held onto guys who weren't good for me for far too long. I ignored the red flags and/or the signs. I gave these guys way too much power over me and now I want to help women who are in the same situation take their power back. No more staring at their phone waiting for a guy who said he'd call or text and doesn't. No more giving him multiple chances when he cancels a date more than once. No more putting their life on hold because of what a guy says but never follows through. Actions speak more truth than words do and women need to understand that."

"So why the singles mixer?" I asked.

"Just trying to get inside the heads of men and find out the reasons behind why they do what they do."

The cab pulled up to her apartment building and she climbed out.

"Thank you for dinner," she spoke.

"You're welcome. You have some great ideas and I'm excited about this shoot. I'll be by at five a.m." I winked.

"I'll be ready and waiting. Have a good night, Mr. Blake."

"You too, Miss Moore."

She shut the door and walked inside the building. There was so much more to her than I'd imagined and I knew I had my work cut out for me if I wanted to win her over. I wanted to text Digits to see what she had to say about the evening. However, I decided to wait at least an hour before messaging her.

#Delete

Chapter Twenty-Seven

Eloise

I opened the door to my apartment with a smile on my face. The evening went well and I enjoyed spending it with Christian. The more I opened up to him about my life, the more comfortable I felt. He was easy to talk to and I was pretty excited about the Chicago trip. But I was also nervous. What I was nervous about, I wasn't sure. Again, he kept the evening strictly professional. I admired him for that because he seemed to respect my boundaries. There was no flirting and no attempt of a kiss.

As I was packing my suitcase, my phone dinged with a text message from Mobile Man.

"Hi. Is your business dinner over?"

"Hi. Yes. I'm just packing for my trip tomorrow. You're home from your date already?"

"Yes. I have an early meeting tomorrow."

"And? How did it go?"

"It went great. I couldn't have asked for a better night or a better person to spend it with. Tell me how your business dinner went."

"It went well. I had a good time."

"This meeting wasn't with that guy you were telling me about, was it? The one you're doing some freelance work for?"

"As a matter of fact, it was." I sent the sad face emoji.

"Why the sad face?"

"Because it's getting harder not to fall for him. I know what you're going to say, so please don't."

"Okay. I won't. You need to do what's right for you, Digits. But just let things happen naturally. If you're meant to be with this guy, then you can't fight it. You can't fight fate."

"You believe in fate, Mobile Man?"

"I do. Just like it was fate that you sent me that very first text. Now look at us. This guy was put in your life for a reason, maybe it wouldn't be so bad to see what that reason is."

"It's getting late and I have to finish packing and get some sleep. Catch ya later?"

"Catch ya later, Digits. Good night and have a safe trip."

"Good night, Mobile Man. Thank you!"

****

"First class?" I arched my brow at Christian.

"It's the only way to fly." He smirked.

Shortly after the plane took off, and while Christian and I were eating our breakfast, a woman walked over to our seats.

"Excuse me. You're Eloise, aren't you?" She smiled.

#Delete

"I am."

"Oh my God. I told my friend it was you. I'm Katherine and I'm a huge fan." She held out her hand in excitement.

"It's nice to meet you, Katherine."

"I just love your blog and that video you posted yesterday on ghosting was phenomenal. I recently went through it and it was devastating. But after watching your video, I can't even tell you how much better and more confident I feel. Thank you." Tears sprang to her eyes.

"Katherine, that's so sweet. Thank you."

"Please tell me you're going to do more videos."

"I am. In fact, I'm going to edit one after breakfast and hopefully get it up today."

"I'm looking forward to it." She grinned. "Are you with him?" she asked as she pointed to Christian.

"Yes. I'm doing some freelance work for his advertising agency."

"Oh. So you're not—" She wiggled her finger back and forth.

"Dating? No." I smiled.

"He's so hot," she mouthed and gave me a wink. "I can't wait to tell everyone I met you. I'll leave you to your breakfast so you can hurry up and get that video posted."

I gave her a smile, and when she walked away, Christian glanced over at me.

"Looks like you're a celebrity."

"Pfft." I waved my hand in front of my face.

He let out a chuckle and continued eating his breakfast.

We arrived in Chicago, and by time we got to the Sofitel Hotel, it was ten thirty.

"Why did we get here so early if check-in isn't until three o'clock and we aren't meeting the people from Chanel until tonight?" I asked with curiosity.

"Why not? Don't you want to explore Chicago?" Christian smiled.

"Of course."

The man behind the lobby desk clicked away at his computer and looked at Christian.

"Actually, Mr. Blake. Your rooms are ready now if you'd like to take your luggage up. You're in rooms 3212 and 3213."

"Perfect." Christian smiled.

We took the elevator up to the thirty-second floor. Once we arrived at our rooms, Christian stopped in front of the door and looked at me.

"Which room do you want?"

"I don't care. Which one do you want?"

"It doesn't matter to me. Both rooms are the same."

"I have an idea." I smiled. "Hold the key cards out in front of you."

I placed my hand over my eyes and took one from his hands.

"Looks like I'm in room 3213," I spoke as I inserted the card into the lock and opened the door. "Let me freshen up and then we can hit the streets of Chicago."

"Sounds good. Just knock on the adjoining door when you're ready."

I entered my room and looked around as I set my bags on the king size bed. The décor was very urban chic with a beige and red theme. I stood in front of the window and took in the amazing city view. Pulling my phone from my purse, I sent Mobile Man a picture.

"Room view. What do you think?"

"I think it's beautiful. Have a good time while you're there and don't sweat the small stuff, Digits."

"Thanks, Mobile Man. I won't. We're getting ready to hit the streets and explore Chicago. Catch ya later?"

"Catch ya later."

I unpacked my makeup bag and took it into the bathroom to freshen up. Once I was done, I knocked on the adjoining door to our rooms. Christian opened it with a smile on his face and my knees went weak.

"Are you ready?" he asked.

"Are you?" I smirked.

"I'm always ready." His cunning smile sent butterflies down below.

We left the hotel and started along the Magnificent Mile. It was a beautiful fall day. Not too warm and not too cool. Just a perfect seventy-one degrees without a cloud in the sky.

"We need to stop in Bloomingdale's," Christian spoke.

"I like Bloomingdale's." I smiled. "Is there something specific you need to get?"

"Some more cologne. In fact, I'm thinking you should pick some up too."

Shit. His cologne drove me insane as it was. He always smelled like he just stepped out of men's magazine.

"I don't need any perfume," I spoke.

"I don't either, but if we're doing a shoot for Chanel, I think it would be a good idea to purchase their cologne/perfume and wear it."

"Ah." I nodded. "I get what you're saying. Wear the scent and get inspired."

"Yes." He gave me a wink.

We stepped into Bloomingdale's and headed towards the Chanel counter.

"May I help you?" The older and attractive woman behind the counter asked with a smile as she looked at Christian.

"I'm interested in Chanel cologne for men." He graciously smiled back and I rolled my eyes.

She grabbed two different bottles from the display and set them in front of us.

"These are our most popular."

#Delete

Christian picked up the bottle labeled Allure Homme Sport and I picked up the bottle of Bleu de Chanel.

"What do you think?" he asked as he held the bottle of Allure up to my nose.

"That one is nice, but so is this one."

"Hmm. That smells bold," he spoke.

"The question is which one does your girlfriend like better?" The sales woman smiled.

"I'm not his girlfriend. We work together, so it doesn't matter which one I like."

"I think it does." Christian smirked at me in a flirtatious way.

I tightened my legs to stop the fierce ache that resided inside me. The ache that only he could satisfy. *Shit.* I hated this and I hated him for doing it to me.

"If I were you, I would go with Bleu de Chanel. You seem like a bold man and you should be wearing a bold fragrance." The sales woman grinned.

"Okay. I'll take it."

I sighed as I walked over to the women's perfume and picked up each bottle and smelled the wonderful fragrance that came from each of them.

"Find one you like?" Christian asked as he walked over to me.

"I like Chanel Chance." I smiled as I held my wrist up to him.

"Very sexy. And I don't just mean the scent." He smirked.

A heat rose in my body. All these perfume smells were creating a sexual tension between us that terrified me. I swallowed hard as I stared into his eyes.

"Thank you."

"No need to thank me when I'm only telling the truth." He winked.

His winks had to stop. My body couldn't take it anymore. I wanted sex. I needed sex. I already knew how sex with him was and I wanted it again. Damn it! I was horny and I knew it was going to get me into trouble.

#Delete

Chapter Twenty-Eight

Eloise

After browsing around Bloomingdale's, we stepped out of the store and continued our shopping spree. We needed to cross the street because I wanted to go to the American Girl store and look at a doll for Hannah's birthday that was coming up. As we approached a crosswalk, we only had five seconds left to cross.

"Come on," Christian spoke as he grabbed my hand.

"No way. We won't make it."

"We will." He smiled as we ran across the street, my hand in his.

We made it to the other side just as the stop signal appeared.

"Told you we'd make it," he spoke. "Life is all about taking chances."

"Taking a chance to get killed?" I arched my brow at him.

He chuckled as my hand was still locked in his. I looked down and then up at him. A feeling between us was felt as he gave me a small smile and let go.

"So why are we going into the American Girl store?" he asked.

"My friend Scarlett has a little girl named Hannah and her birthday is coming up. I'd love to get her one of those bitty babies to play with."

We walked into the store and looked around at all the American Girl Dolls that were on display.

"Wow. This store is very— girly," Christian spoke.

"On my eighth birthday, my parents took me to the one in New York on Fifth Avenue. I thought they brought me there to pick out a doll, but when we walked into the store, we were escorted to the private dining room where my parents had arranged a birthday party for me and eight of my girlfriends."

"You must have been very surprised."

"I was. They took me over to the table, and when I sat down in my chair, my mom handed me a big box. I'll never forget the feeling inside me when I opened that box and inside was an American Girl doll who looked just like me."

"Did she have a name?" Christian asked.

"I named her Maggie. We celebrated my birthday with my friends and our dolls and after, my mom and dad took me around the store and let me pick out two outfits for her. She was my best friend and I divulged my deepest and darkest secrets to her." I smiled.

"Do you still have her?"

"No. When I was fourteen, my parents and I were out to dinner when we got a call from our neighbor that our home was on fire. We lost just about everything, including Maggie."

"I'm sorry, Eloise." He lightly touched my arm.

#Delete

I looked over at him with a small smile.

"Thank you. I was devastated and it took me a long time to get over it. To be honest, I'm not sure that I am. This is the first time since losing her that I've stepped inside an American Girl store. I know it sounds weird."

"Just a little, but I won't hold it against you." He smiled.

We found the section with the Bitty Babies and I picked one out. Glancing over at the outfits, I asked Christian to help me.

"Which one do you like?" I asked.

"For the doll?"

"Of course for the doll." I laughed.

"This two-piece set with the cat on it is cute. Oh look, it comes with matching cat slippers." He smiled as he held them up.

"Those are pajamas."

"So? Do you really think a two-year-old will know the difference?" He smirked.

"It is cute." I picked up the outfit and looked at it. "Good choice, Mr. Blake."

"I do have good taste, and not just in doll clothes." He winked.

A flutter erupted in my belly. We walked up to the counter and I set the doll and pajamas down.

"Hello." The sales girl behind the counter smiled. "Your daughter is going to love this. How old is she?"

"Oh, it's—" I began to speak.

"She's two," Christian spoke up. "She's an absolute angel. I'll never forget the day she was born. It was the best day of my life."

"That's sweet." She grinned at him as I stared in disbelief.

"She's the apple of my eye. Daddy's little girl," Christian spoke.

"Is she here with you?" the sales girl asked.

"No. She's back home." Christian put his arm around me. "We're on a little romantic getaway."

"Aw, that's sweet."

I pulled out my credit card and handed it to her. After I signed, she handed Christian the bag.

"Thank you and enjoy the rest of your romantic getaway." She smiled.

"Oh we will."

We walked out of the store and I stopped on the sidewalk and gave Christian a swift slap on his chest.

"Why did you do that?"

"Ouch. Why not? I don't understand why people just assume things. She should have asked who the doll was for, not just jumped to the conclusion that it was for our daughter."

"We don't have a daughter!"

"Exactly! Anyway, you have to admit it was a little fun to play along." He smiled.

#*Delete*

I didn't respond because I didn't want him to know that it kind of turned me on.

"I'm hungry. Are you?" he asked.

"Yeah. I am."

"Good. Let's go get some lunch. I know this great place. It's not too far from here."

"I hope you're talking about the Grand Lux Café," I spoke.

"I am. You know the place?"

"One of my favorite Chicago restaurants." I smiled. "The last time I was there was with the girls about two years ago."

"It's one of my favorites too."

We enjoyed lunch, talked, laughed, and then headed back to the hotel.

"I think I'm going to take a nap," I spoke. "I'm tired from being up so early and I feel like we might have a late night."

"A nap sounds good. I think I'll take one too," Christian spoke.

As we approached our rooms, Christian glanced over at me.

"Have a nice nap." He smiled.

"You too."

I opened the door and stepped inside. Setting my bag down on the floor, I changed out of my clothes and into the comfy white robe that was hanging in the closet. I was thirsty, so I opened the mini fridge and took out a can of Coke. I needed ice. I couldn't drink pop without it. Grabbing the ice bucket, I

181

opened the door and looked down the hallway to make sure nobody was around. The room where the ice was located was only a few doors down. I filled the bucket and headed back to my room. *Oh shit.* I forgot my key. Sighing, I lightly knocked on Christian's door. He answered it wearing only a pair of gray sweatpants. My senses heightened as I could still smell that damn Chanel cologne on him. I gulped more than once as he stood there and smiled at me.

"May I ask why you're standing in the hallway in a robe?"

"I went to get some ice and forgot my key, so I need to enter my room through your room."

"Oh. Come on in." He waved his hand. "What are you planning on using the ice for?" He smirked.

"My pop." I arched my brow at him. "What else would I use it for?"

"I don't know. Ice can be used in many different ways for many things." A cunning smile crossed his lips.

I felt like I was going to hyperventilate as I opened the adjoining door.

"Enjoy your ice, Miss Moore."

I glared at him from across the room as he chuckled and shut the door. I put some ice into my glass, poured some pop into it, and took a few sips before lying down. I made myself comfortable on the bed and closed my eyes. Images of Christian moved through my head, sending an ache so fierce down below that I couldn't take it anymore.

"Fuck it," I said as I jumped out of bed.

#Delete

Walking over to the adjoining door, I knocked on it and Christian stood there and looked at me.

"Something wrong?" he asked.

I threw myself at him and locked my lips on his. He placed his hands on each side of my face as our kiss continued.

"Are you sure?" he asked me as he broke our kiss.

"Just shut up before I change my mind."

His hands untied my robe and he slid it off my shoulders while our lips tangled together. Laying me down on the bed, he hovered over me and broke our kiss as his eyes burned into mine.

"This is just sex," I spoke. "Only sex."

"I agree. Just sex," he moaned as his lips traveled to my breasts.

His tongue slid over my hardened nipples before his lips wrapped tightly around each one. My breath hitched as tingling sensations soared through my body. The arousal down below was savage and it felt like an orgasm was ready to explode. Moans escaped me as his mouth slid down my torso and navigated its way down to my clit. The soft strokes of his tongue against me made my body tremble and an orgasm to erupt that sent my head spinning out of control.

"That didn't take long." He smiled as he looked up at me.

It didn't matter to him that I already came because he continued to explore me, not only with his mouth but with his fingers. His tongue focused on my clit while he dipped a finger inside me. A jolt of ecstasy opened the gates to a whole new world. A world of sensations that I'd never felt before. How the fuck was this possible? When he was satisfied and done exploring, he stood up and pulled down his sweatpants. The sight of his beautiful cock once again elated me. I quivered at the sight of it, already knowing the pleasure it gave me once before. I lay there in anticipation while he tore open a condom and rolled it on. He slowly climbed on top and hovered over me. After gently kissing my lips, he pushed a strand of my hair from my face, and with a smile, he spoke, "We're going to take it slow this time." I trembled beneath him as his lips softly pressed against the flesh of my neck. My arms wrapped tightly around him as he pushed himself inside me. Slow, steady, and rhythmic with each orgasm-inducing thrust. I threw my head back at the happiness my body felt while his lips caressed mine.

Soft moans erupted from his throat as he moved in and out while my nails dug into his back.

"God, you feel so good," he whispered in my ear.

"So do you," I spoke with bated breath.

He sat back, placed his hands firmly on my hips, and picked up the pace, hitting all the right spots as my body prepared to dive into oblivion. My sensual sounds heightened, and I placed my hands on his firm and muscular chest. The inevitable happened and a second orgasm took over my body, sending a rush not only through me, but also to Christian. His grip tightened as he halted deep inside me, straining, moaning, and fully reveling in a moment of pure joy.

He collapsed on top of me, his hands on each side of my head, softly stroking my hair with his thumbs. Our breathing was out of control and our rapid heartbeats struggled to get back to normal. I lay there, underneath him, our sweaty bodies pressing against one another, reminding us of the pleasure we had just given each other.

"So much for our naps," he spoke with a sense of humor as he rolled off me and removed the condom.

"Right?" I tried to make light of the now awkward situation as I sat up holding the sheet against me.

I watched his hot naked body walk across the room and into the bathroom to dispose of the condom. I climbed off the bed and slipped on my robe while he stood in the doorway of the bathroom and stared at me with a smile on his face.

"I should go take a shower," I nervously spoke as I pointed to my room.

"Yeah. I should too. We need to be downstairs in the restaurant at six o'clock."

I gave him a small smile and stepped into my room. With my hand on the handle, getting ready to pull the door shut, I looked at him.

"It was only sex, Christian. Nothing else."

"I know, Eloise. No worries."

Chapter Twenty-Nine

Christian

I stepped into the shower, the smell of her all over my body and her taste on my lips. I smiled as I leaned my head back under the mist of the hot water, letting the warmth run down my face. Sex with her was undeniably the ultimate experience as far as I was concerned. She said it was only sex, but I knew damn well it was more than that to her. I felt it in the way her hands roamed my body. I felt it in the way her nails dug into my back and I felt it with each sensual sound she let out. For me, it was more than just sex, and as far as I was concerned, I was one step closer to having her.

While we were at lunch, she began asking questions about my parents and childhood. I needed to be careful with what I said because I had already told her, aka Digits, a lot. I couldn't risk her finding out it was me she was actually talking to. Not yet. But with each passing day, it was becoming harder and harder not to. Digits and I were growing closer. Maybe I needed to cut it off with her and let some time pass. Maybe Eloise would never have to know. That was something I needed to carefully think about.

After my shower, I sat down on the bed with my phone in my hand and thought about texting Digits. Then I decided not to. As I got up to put on my clothes, my phone dinged with a text message from her.

"Hi."

"Hi. How's your trip going?"

"Good. How's your day? Is work busy?"

"Work is always busy. Other than that, my day is great."

"Good to hear. I just wanted to say hi."

"Everything okay, Digits?"

"Yeah. Things are good. I need to get ready for dinner. Catch ya later?"

"Catch ya later. If you want to talk tonight, text me, no matter what time it is."

"Thanks, Mobile Man. I will."

I sighed as I set my phone down and got ready for dinner. When I knocked on our adjoining door, Eloise opened it and I stood there in awe at the sight of her. A beautiful nude-colored short dress, delicately beaded, sat off her shoulders and hugged her petite hourglass figure. Her long brown hair was twisted up into an elegant hair-do with a few curls that hung down. I let out an approving whistle as I tried to calm down my misbehaving cock.

"You look stunning." I smiled. "Are you ready?"

"Thank you. Almost. I just have to put on my heels and then we can go." She smiled as she grabbed her shoes and sat down on the edge of the bed.

I couldn't stop staring at her long, lean legs as she slipped her feet into her nude-colored heels. The way she had had them wrapped tightly around my waist as I fucked her was intoxicating.

"Now I'm ready," she spoke.

I placed my hand on the small of her back as she picked up her purse from the dresser and we walked out of the room. A smile crossed my lips when I felt her tremble at the subtle touch of my hand.

We took the elevator down to the restaurant where my friend, Joe, was standing and waiting for us.

"Christian, good to see you, my friend." We lightly hugged.

"Good to see you too. Joe, I'd like you to meet Eloise Moore, our photographer. Eloise, this is Joe."

"It's nice to meet you." She smiled as she placed her hand in his.

"And you as well." Joe nodded.

He led us to a table where three other people, including the two models, from Chanel sat. We ate, drank, and talked mostly about business. After dinner was finished, we stayed for a couple more drinks and then headed up to our rooms.

"Good night, Eloise," I spoke before walking into my room.

"Good night, Christian. See you in the morning."

I closed the door and set my keycard on the night stand. As I looked at my bed, I wished I was seeing her lying in it next to me.

****

#Delete

Eloise

I opened my suitcase, changed into my nightshirt, and took out my small travel bag. Taking it into the bathroom, I took out my toothbrush but noticed my toothpaste wasn't there. After looking through my suitcase and realizing I must have left it at home, I walked over to the adjoining door and knocked on it.

"Everything okay?" Christian asked as he opened the door and his half naked body instantly aroused me.

"Can I borrow your toothpaste? I left mine at home."

"Sure. I'll go get it for you."

He walked away and I stared at the bed where we had sex earlier in the day.

"Here you go." He smiled as he handed me the tube.

"Thanks. Hold on a sec and I'll bring it right back."

"You know, we could always just keep this door open in case there's anything else you need. That way, you wouldn't have to knock."

"And what else would I need?" I narrowed my eye at him as I handed him back his toothpaste.

"Oh, I don't know." He smirked.

"Good night, Mr. Blake." I began to shut the door.

"Good night, Miss Moore. You know where to find me if you need me."

"I won't need you!" I shouted from the other side of the door.

After brushing my teeth, I climbed into bed and lay there,

eyes wide open. I was exhausted so why couldn't I sleep? Maybe it was because every time I closed my damn eyes, all I saw was Christian. I grabbed my phone from the nightstand and sent a text message to Mobile Man.

"We had sex again and this time I initiated it from lack of control."

"Lol. Good for you, Digits!"

"It's not funny, Mobile Man."

"I'm sorry. Of course it's not funny. Do you regret it?"

"No. I can't even explain to you how he makes me feel."

"Why don't you try?"

"It was different this time."

"How?"

"I don't know how to put it into words. It felt like our souls merged. Like we both connected on a level deeper that I never knew existed or experienced before."

"That's good, right? I think something like that is rare to find or experience."

"I don't know. I basically attacked him and I feel ashamed."

"Did he enjoy it?"

"Of course he enjoyed it. What man wouldn't enjoy a woman practically attacking him for sex?"

"Lol. True."

"What he must think of me."

#Delete

"Do you want my thoughts on that?"

"Yes, please."

"He more than likely thinks you're a beautiful woman who knows what she wants and goes after it. That's a huge turn on for men."

"Ha. Tell that to all the losers I dated. I think they were more intimidated by me than anything."

"That's why they're all losers, Digits. A weak man can't handle a strong woman because he doesn't know what to do with her, but a strong man loves the challenges of a strong woman. And I do believe this guy you've had sex with twice now is a strong man who knows what he wants. Hence, not a loser. Listen, don't get all caught up in what he thinks about you because your animal instincts took over. I'm pretty sure your sexiness level blew off the charts in his eyes."

"Thanks, Mobile Man. I'm going to head to bed now. It was a long day and I'm tired."

"Sleep well, Digits. Catch ya later."

"You too. Catch ya later."

Chapter Thirty

Eloise

My eyes flew open at the sound of my alarm going off, waking me from the dream I was in the middle of. A dream that consisted of me and Christian rolling around in crisp white sheets as the ocean air blew through the window of our room, leaving me with a feeling of an unfinished orgasm.

"Shit," I whispered to myself as I sat up in bed.

I sighed as I hopped into the shower and got ready for the photo shoot, leaving very little time to finish off what he had started in my dream. I wasn't going to let this affect me. I wasn't going to let him affect me. I needed full concentration for the shoot and I couldn't afford any distractions. Just him being there would be distraction enough. While I was putting on my makeup, there was a light knock on the adjoining door. Walking over, I opened it and there stood Christian with a tube of toothpaste in one hand and a cup of coffee in the other.

"Good morning. I figured you needed both of these." He grinned.

"Good morning. I definitely do. Thank you."

I took the coffee and the toothpaste from him and went back into the bathroom.

#Delete

"I took the liberty of ordering breakfast for us," he spoke. "It should be here shortly."

"Thank you. I'm starving. Are we going to have time to eat?" I asked as I looked at the time on my phone.

"We'll have to eat fast," he replied.

He left the adjoining door open and went back into his room. From where the bathroom was positioned, I could see part of his room in the mirror. I kept glancing as I twisted strands of my hair around the barrel of my curling iron. I could see him standing there putting on his watch and then he took a seat on the edge of the bed and slipped on his shoes. The ache down below that never fully went away grew stronger. Just looking at him reminded me of the intense dream I had. It was one of those dreams that would stay with me for a while.

Just as I finished getting ready, there was knock on the door. Christian walked over and answered it while I put on my shoes.

"Breakfast is served," he spoke as he took the silver tray over to the small round table with two chairs that sat in the corner.

Right when I sat down to eat, my phone rang and it was Claire calling.

"Hello," I answered.

"Have you seen your blog and your YouTube channel since you posted those videos?" she asked.

"No. I haven't had a chance to look."

"Tell Claire I said hi," Christian whispered from across the table.

"Well, you need to look right now!"

"Christian said hi," I spoke. "And why? What's going on?"

"Tell him I said hi. Just look, Eloise!" she demanded.

"Okay. Okay."

I got up from the table and grabbed my laptop from the bed. Logging into my blog, I sat there and stared at it with my eyes popped out of my head. My subscribers had reached over a million and my videos had over five hundred thousand views. Clicking over to my YouTube channel, I already had over seventy thousand subscribers and each video I posted had over fifty thousand views so far.

"Oh my God, Claire!"

"I know, right? When you get a chance, read the comments! I think you're onto something here with #Delete, Eloise."

"Thank you for letting me know. I'm so excited!"

"You're welcome. Good luck with the shoot today and call me later!"

"I will. Bye."

I inhaled a deep breath and let it out as I looked at Christian.

"Congratulations." He smiled.

"Thank you. I honestly can't believe it."

"I do believe a celebration is in order tonight. You in?" He winked.

"Sure. I'm in." I smiled.

The photo shoot took approximately seven hours. Between the street shots, hotel shots, navy pier shots, and numerous dress changes, I didn't expect it to take any less time.

"Great job, Eloise. How long until we can get the proofs?" Joe asked.

"Thanks, Joe. I can have them mailed out to you as early as next Thursday. Will that work for you?"

"I'm actually going to be in New York on Thursday, so just bring them by Christian's office. Let's say around one o'clock. I'll have Christian order us in some lunch and we can view them together."

"Sounds good." I smiled.

"It was nice meeting you, Eloise. I look forward to seeing those pictures. Have a safe trip home."

"Thank you."

After Christian said goodbye to Joe and the rest of the Chanel staff, he walked over to me as I was packing up my camera equipment.

"You were amazing today," he spoke.

"Thanks. Everyone was super nice and easy to work with. Especially the models. Sometimes they can be quite difficult." I smirked.

"I bet they can be. I'm sure you want to shower before heading to dinner."

"I do. Being a photographer can get pretty dirty."

"You were on the ground an awful lot." He laughed. "Reservations are for eight."

We took a cab back to the hotel and Christian followed me into my room and set one of the equipment bags he carried down on the table.

"I'm going to go change. Just let me know when you're ready," he spoke.

"I will. This celebration we're doing, is it fancy or casual?"

"Casual." He winked as he started to walk to his room. "By the way." He turned and looked at me. "I hope you're not afraid of heights."

Before I could get any words out, he walked to his room and shut the door. What the hell did he mean by that? I wasn't a fan of heights. Now I was worried. I took a quick shower, and when I got out, I sat down on the bed with my laptop and began looking through the hundreds of emails from women around the world. As much as I loved photography, I loved helping women more. It was at that moment while reading the emails that I decided to take a break from photography and make my blog and YouTube channel a priority. It was a risk. A huge risk. But, like someone told me, "Some of the greatest gifts in life are on the other side of fear."

I picked up my phone and sent a text message to Mobile Man.

"We didn't touch base today. How are you?"

"I'm great. How are you? I was wondering if I'd hear from you. I didn't want to bother you because I knew you were busy."

"I'm good. I had a really good day and now I need to get ready to go to dinner."

"How are things going between the two of you?"

#Delete

"Things are going good. Maybe too good. The part that sucks is that he's always on my mind even when we're not together."

"Why does that suck?"

"Because I don't want to think about him. I don't need the distraction, but I can't help it."

"Listen to me, Digits. You can try to fight your feelings for this guy all you want, but you'll lose and you know it. That's why I think you're so scared. Just give in to those feelings. Obviously, the guy feels the same way about you. Take it slow. One day at a time. Open yourself up to the possibility that this guy is the exception of all other men."

"You think?"

"I know. I spent the day with the woman of my dreams today. And you know why? Because I took your advice. Take your own advice, Digits. If you like him, let him know. Because one day, you'll wake up and he won't be there and then you'll spend the rest of your life wondering what could have been."

"Thank you, Mobile Man. Have I ever told you how much I love our conversations?"

"I'm sure you have and I love them too. Conversations with you are the highlight of my day." He sent the winky face.

I sent him the winky face back and told him to have a good night. My feelings about him and our text friendship were starting to change. He met the woman of his dreams already, so him falling for me wasn't even a consideration. Maybe it was time me and Mobile Man met. Maybe a man and a woman could just be friends.

Chapter Thirty-One

Christian

There was a knock on the adjoining door, and when I opened it, I smiled as I saw Eloise standing there looking as gorgeous as ever.

"Are you ready?" I asked.

"I am. Where are we going?"

"You'll see when we get there." I smiled.

I rented out the Skydeck Chicago for the two of us, a private dining experience on the 103rd floor. I'd had dinner there once before with my family and it was an amazing experience. An experience I wanted to share with her. I wanted to make this a night she'd never forget, and with any luck, she'd be waking up in my arms in the morning.

When we arrived and stepped into the elevator, I could see the look of nervousness across her face.

"Are you okay?" I lightly grabbed hold of her hand.

She looked down and then up at me.

"I am now." She lightly smiled.

A feeling of contentment washed over me hearing her say

#Delete

those words. I was breaking through to her. Maybe my last text message as Mobile Man got her thinking. When we arrived to the 103rd floor, we stepped out and she looked around, her hand tightly clenched in mine.

"I really hope you're not afraid of heights because this is something everyone should experience in their lifetime," I spoke.

She took in a deep breath.

"It's not that I'm really afraid. I'm just unsure. Why are we the only two people up here?"

"I rented out the entire room for us so we could have a private dinner and enjoy the view in peace." I smiled. "Come over here and look out at the city."

"Umm. I'm not sure I want to get too close to the glass." She stopped behind me.

"It's okay, Eloise. I have you and I promise I won't let go." I smiled.

****

Eloise

My heart was beating a hundred miles a minute. No wait, make that a thousand miles a minute. Not only because our hands were locked together, but because we were up really high and I wasn't sure how to deal with the anxiety I felt. I couldn't believe he rented out the entire Skydeck for the two of us. That had to be the sweetest thing anyone had ever done for me. After taking in a couple of deep breaths, I let him lead me to the window.

"What's that?"

"That's the ledge."

"You mean people actually walk on it?"

"Yes." He chuckled. "Would you like to give it a try?"

"Nope. I'm good right here."

We took a seat at a round table where a bottle of wine sat. After Christian took the seat across from me, he poured us each a glass of wine.

"Dinner will be served shortly." He grinned. "Here's to a successful photo shoot and to your successful blog." He held up his glass.

"Thank you." I smiled big as I clanked my glass against his. "So, tell me again why you're single?"

"Oh, I don't know. Maybe the right woman hasn't popped into my life. You do have to be careful whom you choose to want to spend the rest of your life with." He smirked.

"True. So you want marriage and a family?"

"One day in the future. That's if the right woman comes along and sweeps me off my feet." He winked and my lady parts quivered.

I gave him a small smile as the waiter walked over and served us dinner.

"It really is beautiful up here. Thank you," I spoke as the anxiety seemed to have dissipated.

"You're welcome."

#*Delete*

We ate, talked about the photo shoot, and when dinner was over, music from the overhead started to play. Christian got up from his chair and held out his hand to me.

"May I have this dance? The night wouldn't be complete without dancing on the skydeck." He smiled.

I placed my napkin from my lap onto the table and put my hand in his.

"We're going to dance on the ledge and I don't want you to be afraid," he spoke.

A nervousness settled in the pit of my stomach.

"Do you trust me, Eloise?" he asked with seriousness as his eyes stared into mine.

"I think so."

He let out a chuckle.

"You think so?"

"Yes, of course I do."

With our hands clasped together, he led me to the ledge and I gulped.

"It's okay. I've got you."

We stepped onto the ledge and he wrapped his arm securely around my waist as I placed my hand in his and my other hand on his shoulder. We swayed back and forth to the music as I looked out at the brightly lit city from the 103rd floor.

"Are you okay?" Christian asked.

"Actually, I'm fine. It's beautiful up here." I smiled. "And you're right, this is something everyone should experience in their lifetime."

"I'm glad you like it. I somehow knew you would." He smiled.

He let go of my hand and wrapped his other arm around me. Bringing both arms up, I secured them around his neck as the two of us stared at each other, getting lost in one another's soul. The corners of his mouth were slightly curved into a seductive smile that sent shivers down my spine. He wanted to kiss me. I felt it. And in a matter of seconds, his lips gently pressed against mine. He looked at me and I smiled, letting him know that I was on board with whatever he was thinking about. He leaned in again, but this time, his kiss was more sensual and not just a test. I returned it and our tongues met with satisfaction. His hands roamed up and down my sides as mine tangled through his hair. If we didn't leave now, we'd end up having sex on the ledge. Would that really be so bad? I was sure the staff would mind.

"Shall we go back to the hotel?" he asked as he broke our kiss.

"Yes." I swallowed hard.

With a grin on his face, he took my hand and we left the Skydeck. Our hands never left each other's all the way back to the hotel. Once we stepped into the elevator, and being the only ones in there, he pushed me up against the wall and savagely kissed me as we traveled from floor to floor. The doors opened and he grabbed my hand and led us to our rooms.

"Which room? Mine or yours?" he asked.

"Yours is fine." I smiled.

#Delete

He inserted the cardkey, opened the door, and swept me up in his arms and over to the bed where we made passionate love. I lay there, wrapped in his arms, my head on his chest and his finger stroking my bare skin.

"I want to see you on a regular basis when we get back to New York," he spoke.

Fear and confusion rose inside me. I gave serious thought to what Mobile Man said about just letting go and spending the rest of my life wondering what could have been. Christian Blake was everything I was looking for in a man and my intuition was telling me to go for it. I failed at listening to my intuition before, but this time, I knew better.

"I'd like to see you too." I lifted my head and looked at him.

"Really?" A smile grew across his face.

"Yes, really."

With one swift move, I was flat on my back and Christian was hovering over me.

Chapter Thirty-Two

Christian

I'd won and I couldn't have been happier, but a darkness resided deep inside me. I couldn't sleep when I should have been sleeping like a baby. I had it all. I had her. I sat on the edge of the bed with my face buried in my hands thinking about how I was going to tell her that I was Mobile Man. I didn't know how she'd react and that was what scared me the most.

"Hey, are you okay?" she asked as she placed her hand on my back.

"I'm fine. I'm sorry I woke you."

"You didn't. Why aren't you asleep?"

"I don't know. Maybe too much excitement from the day."

I climbed back under the sheets, wrapped her up in my arms, and kissed her head.

"Go back to sleep, baby. I'm fine. I promise."

I awoke the next morning to the sound of rain hitting the window.

"I love the sound of the rain," she softly spoke.

"Me too. Good morning." I kissed her head.

#Delete

"Good morning." Her lips pressed against my chest. "What time does our flight leave?"

"Not until six o'clock tonight. I didn't think they were calling for rain today. The last time I checked the weather, there was a zero percent chance."

"A little bit of rain never hurt anybody." She smiled as she looked up at me. "I'll be right back. Don't go anywhere." She kissed me before climbing out of bed and slipping into her robe.

She opened the adjoining door to her room, and after a few seconds, she came back with her camera in her hand.

"What are you doing?" I laughed.

"I'm going to take some pictures of you. That is, if you don't mind."

"In bed?" I cocked my head as her camera went off.

"Yes. It's sexy and I like sexy." She grinned.

She stood on top of the bed and began snapping pictures while looking down.

"Get down here." I grabbed her legs and pulled her on top of me. "No more pictures. If you want sexy, I'll give you sexy." I kissed her.

Slipping her robe off her shoulders, I took her beautiful breasts in my mouth. My hard cock was pressed against her and waiting to feel the warmth of her insides. She lifted herself up and slowly pushed down until every inch of me was inside her. Subtle moans escaped both our lips as we took in the pleasure we gave each other.

"We're not using a condom?" I asked.

"I'm on birth control. I'm not worried."

I placed my hands firmly on her breasts, lightly pinching each hardened peak as she slowly rode my cock. I threw my head back in satisfaction as the warmth inside her enveloped me.

"God, you feel incredible."

"So do you," she sensually moaned.

Watching her make love to me was the best turn on in the world. She was so fucking beautiful and I couldn't get enough of her. Her hips moved back and forth at a rapid pace as her moans heightened and she came. The wetness that emerged from her sent a trembling sensation through me. A sensation I couldn't control. A sensation that sent my cock into a spastic fit of an orgasm. I held her hips down firmly as I pushed out every last drop I had inside her.

Before climbing off me, her lips pressed against mine.

"I'm starving." She smiled.

"Me too. Let's get dressed and head down to breakfast."

We kept the adjoining door open and traveled between rooms as we both got dressed. While Eloise was in her bathroom applying her makeup, I walked up from behind and wrapped my arms around her.

"I'm going to head down to the gift shop and grab us a couple umbrellas."

"Good idea. We're going to need them." She smiled.

I left the room and headed towards the elevator. Pulling my phone from my pocket, I sent Digits a text message.

"Good morning. How was your night?"

"Good morning! My night was fabulous. He told me he wants to see me on a regular basis when we get back home."

"That's good. What did you say?"

"I told him that I'd like to see him too."

"I'm proud of you, Digits. So you took my advice?"

"Yes and thank you. I guess I didn't want to spend the rest of my life wondering what could have been."

"I'm happy to hear you say that."

"What about you and the woman of your dreams?"

"I think things are going to work out really well with her."

"Wow. Look at us." I sent the smiley face emoji.

"I have to run, Digits. Have a great day. When are you heading back?"

"Our flight leaves at six p.m."

"Have a safe flight. Catch ya later?"

"Catch ya later, Mobile Man."

I sighed as I stood there and stared at our text messages. This couldn't go on. I either had to tell Eloise who I was or I had to stop texting Digits. Either way, she was going to be hurt and the last thing I wanted to do was hurt her.

Chapter Thirty-Three

Eloise

After Christian and I had breakfast, we headed back to our rooms to pack all our things so we could check out. After leaving our bags with the hotel until we were ready to go to the airport, we stepped onto the rainy streets of Chicago and Christian opened the oversized black umbrella.

"I can't believe they only had one left," I spoke.

"I'm sure a lot of people had the same idea we did when they saw the rain outside. I'm happy this was the last one. It'll keep me closer to you." He winked.

I couldn't help but smile as I laid my head on his shoulder. We shopped for a couple of hours, and even though it was a dreary cool day out, it turned out to be one of the best days of my life. We tried on clothes we would never buy just to be silly and took an obscene number of selfies to remember our time in Chicago. Because we had a huge breakfast, neither one of us was very hungry, so we ended up getting a couple of hot dogs from a street vendor and eating them under an overhang and out of the rain.

"You're a cheap date. I think I like you." Christian smiled.

I nudged his shoulder with mine. "I think I like you too.

#*Delete*

Thanks for the hotdog."

He leaned over and kissed my lips. I couldn't recall a time I was any happier. Once we finished eating, we headed back to the hotel to collect our bags and then it was off to the airport. On the plane ride home, Christian did some work on his laptop while I planned the videos I was going to film for the week.

"I decided to take a break from photography for a while," I spoke as I glanced at Christian.

"Really? Why?"

"My passion right now is with my blog and helping women with their relationship issues. The only thing I have going on next week are the edits for the Chanel photos. I'm not going to accept any more work for probably about a month."

"Can you afford not to take on photography jobs?" he asked.

"Yes." I smiled. "I can afford it."

"Then do what makes you happy." He placed his hand on mine.

As soon as we landed, my phone dinged with a text message from Natalie.

"Are you New York bound yet? I'm back from Hawaii and was hoping we could have a drink or three. I need to talk to you."

"Just landed. I should be home in about an hour. Everything okay?"

"I don't know. I need your advice about Nathan."

"Okay. I'll text you when I'm close to home."

"Thanks. I'll bring the wine."

"Everything okay?" Christian asked.

"Yeah. That was Natalie. She's coming over when I get home. She needs advice about Nathan."

"Is that her boyfriend or husband?"

"Some guy she just met in Hawaii. He lives on Long Island."

Christian had a car waiting at the airport to take us home. When the driver pulled up to my building, Christian got out of the car, grabbed my luggage, and walked me to my apartment. After setting my luggage down in the foyer, he wrapped his arms around me and pulled me into a tight embrace.

"I had a great time in Chicago and I think I'm going to miss you tonight."

"I had a great time too. Thank you for everything. And I think I'm going to miss you too." I smiled.

His lips tenderly brushed against mine and it was turning into a passionate kiss until there was knock at my door.

"I'll text you later." He placed his hands on each side of my face and kissed me one last time.

"I look forward to it."

I opened the door and let Natalie in.

"Oh. Hi, Christian." She smiled.

"Hello, Natalie. How was Hawaii?"

"Beautiful. How was Chicago?"

"Beautiful." He winked at her.

As soon as he left, I shut the door and took the bottle of wine from Natalie's hand.

"So what was he doing up here?" she asked.

"He helped me with my luggage." I grinned.

"You're glowing. What's going on?"

"We're sort of seeing each other," I spoke as I took down two wine glasses.

"As in dating?" Her brow arched.

"I suppose."

"You slept with him again." She smirked.

"I did. A few times." I grinned like a little girl on Christmas morning.

"And you're okay with dating him? Why the sudden change in attitude?"

"He's a great guy, Natalie, and everything I'm looking for. But enough about me and Christian. What's going on?"

"Nathan hasn't returned any of my text messages since he's been home."

"Not one of them?" I asked.

"No," she replied as she downed her glass of wine. "I'm not used to this. I'm usually the one who doesn't text back. I really like him, Eloise, and I thought he liked me too. For fuck sakes, I slept with him."

"Whatever you do, don't text him again. Why was he in Hawaii?"

"Business trip," she replied.

"And he's never been married?"

"He said no."

"How about a girlfriend?"

"He said he hasn't had one in a long time."

"It's possible he *does* have a girlfriend here and she didn't go with him because it was a business trip."

"That little fucker. I swear to god, if that's true..." Her brows furrowed.

She reached inside her purse and pulled out her phone.

"Oh. He just sent me a text message." She grinned.

"What does it say?"

"He said he's sorry he didn't respond but work has been crazy since he got back and he's been practically working 24/7. He wants to take me out tomorrow night."

"On a Monday?" I narrowed my eye at her.

"Better than not at all." She smiled. "I'm sure he misses me."

"I'm sure he does," I spoke to make her feel better.

The truth was, something wasn't sitting right with me and this Nathan guy. Nobody is that busy to take ten seconds to

#Delete

reply to a text message. If things were as great in Hawaii as she said they were, he wouldn't have ignored her. Red flag number one.

When she left, I took my luggage to my room and sat down on the edge of my bed and sent a text message to Mobile Man.

"Hi. I'm back!"

About an hour later, he replied, which was unusual for him.

"Hi. Welcome home. I'm heading to bed. Catch ya later?"

"Sure. Catch ya later."

I sat there and stared at the text message, thinking to myself that he seemed off. Just as I was about to text him and ask if everything was okay, I received a text from Christian.

"Hi. Is it bad to say that I miss you already?"

"Hi. I miss you too."

"Look out your window."

I gave his text message a confused look, got up from my bed, and looked out my bedroom window, only to find Christian standing on the sidewalk in front of my building with a small bag in his hand. Opening the window with a smile, I yelled, "What are you doing?"

"Coming back to see you. That's if you don't mind."

"Of course not. Come on up."

Excitement barreled through me as I ran to the door and opened it, waiting for him to step off the elevator. This was crazy. My feelings were crazy. I was so into him that I couldn't see straight, and the fact that he came back only after just leaving a couple of hours ago meant that he was really into me too.

The elevator dinged, and as soon as he stepped off, I ran to him and wrapped my arms around him.

"Whoa." He chuckled. "I'm happy I came over."

"Me too." I kissed his lips.

We walked back to my apartment and I immediately offered him a glass of wine.

"So you're spending the night?" I bit down on my bottom lip and the corners of my mouth slightly curved upwards into a bashful smile.

"If you'll have me, yes."

"I will definitely have you." I wrapped my arms around his neck.

Chapter Thirty-Four

Eloise

He set down his glass of wine on the counter and brought his hand up to my cheek as his lips softly brushed against mine. My body screamed with excitement for it knew what was to come. He slid my leggings off my hips and pulled my sweater over my head, leaving me in only my bra and panties. He inhaled a sharp breath as he ran his finger down my cleavage. Our mouths smashed together while I undid his belt, took down his pants, and brushed my hand against his hard cock. He broke our kiss, lifted his shirt, and tossed it on the floor. Standing in front of me, his eyes studied me from head to toe.

"You are the most beautiful woman in the world," he softly spoke as he leaned in and swept his lips across my neck.

His hand traveled down the front of my panties, gently stroking my clit before plunging a finger deep inside me. I was already wet. How could I not be? This man turned me on more than any other man ever had. I was in a constant state of wetness when he was around.

He moaned with pleasure as my fingers wrapped themselves around his rock-hard cock and my hand moved up and down his shaft. He explored me, not only with his fingers, but with his warm tongue as he slid across my neck and down to my cleavage. Bringing his free hand around me, he unclasped my bra with ease and let it fall and then took my hardened nipples in his mouth. The sensation that flowed through me was euphoric as I let out several moans of passion. He picked me up and set me on the edge of the island.

"I can't wait anymore," he whispered as he thrust into me.

I gasped for air, wrapping my legs around his waist and leaning back as far as I could so he had access to my breasts. His mouth explored me as his thrusts became rapid, hitting all the right spots that only his cock could hit. After a few more intense thrusts, he picked me up, my arms wrapped tightly around his neck, and held me as he moved in and out of me. His strength was captivating and made me feel completely safe. He carried me to the bedroom and laid me down on the bed, hovering over me and staring into my eyes as he performed like a beast. My heart was pounding as I moaned out in contentment at the orgasm that shook my world.

"That's it. Fuck, yes," he yelled out as he halted deep inside and a rush of warmth filled within me.

Christian collapsed and our bodies meshed together as we both lay there waiting for our breath to return to a normal pattern. He rolled off me and lay on his back with his hands on his chest.

"Are you okay?" I laughed as I ran my finger across his shoulder.

"I'm more than okay." He grinned as he looked at me.

I kissed his lips and climbed off the bed, strutting my naked body into the bathroom.

"Would you care to join me for a bath?" I turned and gave him a sultry look.

#Delete

"I would love to."

We lay together in the bubbly warm water. My back was pressed against his muscular chest and his arms were wrapped securely around me. We talked a lot about my parents and their relationship. One thing that had me concerned was he didn't want to talk about his family. I noticed every time I asked him, he was vague and tried to change the subject.

"Is there something you're not telling me about your family?" I asked.

"No. Why?"

"Because every time I ask you about them, you change the subject."

He sighed. "I don't really want to talk about them right now. We will another time. Okay?"

"Okay." I tilted my head back and looked up at him as he kissed my forehead.

After our bath, we climbed into my bed and I snuggled against Christian as tight as I could. I fit perfectly against his body and laid my head upon his chest, listening to the subtle beat of his heart and the soft whispers of his breath. This had become my happy place.

The next morning, I couldn't sleep, so I got up early and made Christian some waffles.

"What is that delicious smell?" He smiled as he kissed my lips.

"Good morning. I made you some homemade waffles." I grinned.

"I love waffles." He patted my ass.

I poured him a cup of coffee and told him to sit down.

"Can I see you tonight?" he asked.

I placed two waffles on a plate and set it down in front of him. Climbing on his lap, I spoke, "You can see me every night."

"Mhm. I like the sound of that. I'll pick you up on my way home from work and we can have dinner at my place."

"I like your place." I smiled. "Especially your bathroom."

"If you like my bathroom, then you'll love my bedroom even more." His lips brushed against mine.

He finished his breakfast, gave me a kiss goodbye, and headed to the office. After he left, I got to work on editing the Chanel photos. I couldn't stop thinking about Mobile Man and I was surprised I hadn't heard from him today. This wasn't like him not to text me.

"Top of the day to you! How are you?"

I set my phone down and continued editing my photos. About an hour had passed and I still hadn't heard from him, so I sent him another text message.

"Hey, I hope everything is okay."

****

Christian

I sat behind my desk and sighed as I stared at her text message. This was killing me because I knew she was hurting

#Delete

that Mobile Man hadn't responded to her text messages. Finally, I said fuck it, and against my better judgment, I sent her a message back.

"Hey. I'm sorry for the late response. I was tied up in an important meeting. I'm good and everything's fine. How are you?"

"I'm great! I was worried about you last night. You sounded kind of off. Are things going well with that girl?"

"Things couldn't be better with her and I'm really happy. Actually, I'm the happiest I've ever been in my life."

"Aw, that's so good to hear. I wanted to thank you again for your advice. Like you, I'm the happiest I've ever been. He's such an amazing man. He rented out the Skydeck Chicago for the two of us and we had a beautiful dinner together. No one had ever done anything like that for me before."

"Wow. He went all out for you, Digits. And you know why he did it? Because he knows you deserve nothing less."

"Thank you, Mobile Man. That was sweet of you to say."

"I only type the truth. I have another meeting to get to. Catch ya later?"

"Catch ya later."

Just as I set my phone down, Claire walked into my office.

"Hi, I haven't seen you all morning. How was Chicago?"

"Chicago was fantastic. The photo shoot went really well," I spoke.

"I haven't heard from Eloise yet. Did the two of you get

along okay?"

A grin crossed my face. "Yes. We got along just fine."

Her eye narrowed at me in a suspicious way.

"Anything I should know?" She cocked her head.

"Maybe you should wait and talk to her." I smirked.

"No. It's okay. You can tell me."

"We're seeing each other." I placed my hands behind my head and leaned back in my chair.

"That's great." She smiled. "Finally. So how did it go when you told her that you were Mobile Man?"

I stared blankly at her for a moment.

"Oh my god, Christian. You haven't told her yet?" She took a seat across from me.

"It's complicated, Claire."

"Oh, I know how complicated it is. You cannot keep that from her. Do you know what she's going to do to you when she finds out you knew?"

"I think the best way to avoid that is for me to stop texting her as Mobile Man. Just let it go and be done with it."

"That will hurt her. She really likes Mobile Man. You need to come clean to her, Christian. It's not even an option."

"Isn't is better for her to be hurt by someone she's never even met? She'll get over it a lot faster."

She sat there, slowly shaking her head at me.

#Delete

"It's not right. You can't start a relationship based on a lie. And don't give me that 'What she doesn't know won't hurt her' spiel either. Once you tell her, she'll probably be pissed as hell, but Natalie, Scarlett, and I will be there for her and talk to her. We'll have your back because I believe the two of you belong together."

I sighed as I placed my hands on my desk.

"I'll tell her by the end of the week," I spoke with dismay. "But I'm not texting her as Mobile Man anymore. Maybe that way, it won't be so hard on her when she finds out why."

"That's up to you. But it's also up to you to make things right. If you like her as much as you say you do, then you know telling her is the right decision."

"I think I'm falling in love with her," I softly spoke.

"Then tell her."

Claire walked out of my office and I took my stress ball from my desk and threw it across the room.

Chapter Thirty-Five

Eloise

The week was flying by and I couldn't believe it was already Thursday. Since Monday, I had filmed and edited five videos, three of which were already posted and two more scheduled for the next two days. I finished the edits for the Chanel Campaign and had them packaged nicely to take to Christian's office. Christian and I saw each other every night since we we'd been back from Chicago, and last night, he surprised me with a dozen pink and white roses. I asked him what they were for and his answer: "Just because." I was on cloud nine and the happiest I'd ever been. My parents invited us over to dinner on Saturday and I was beyond excited for them to meet him. I knew they were going to love him. As for his texting habits, he was right on point. Always responded within ten minutes or less, and most of the time, he initiated the text messages. Our nightly routine was adorable as far as I was concerned. We'd have sex, he'd kiss me and say good night, and then he would pick up his phone from the nightstand and send me a good night text. I'd look at my phone and then at him and he'd give me that sexy wink that melted my heart.

The text messages between me and Mobile Man started to fade, and not because of me. He would go hours without responding, and when he did, it was usually with one or two words. Our long conversations we used to have suddenly

#Delete

stopped. I spoke to Natalie, Scarlett, and Claire about it, and they said he was probably heartbroken that I'd found someone. I told them to stop being ridiculous because he had a girl of his own, the one he called the love of his life. So it had to be something else. I was really bothered by it because I considered him one of my best friends. I told him things I couldn't tell my girls. He pulled away and I wanted answers. Normally, I would #Delete him, but we'd never met, went out, nothing. We only talked every day via texting, so to me, #Delete didn't apply in this situation. We weren't dating and we weren't interested in each other romantically.

I grabbed the Chanel photos and headed to Christian's office. When I stepped off the elevator, Claire was standing there with Kenny.

"Hey, you two." I smiled.

"Hi, Eloise." Kenny kissed my cheek. "What are you doing here?"

"Dropping these photos off to Christian."

"Ah. Can I talk to you for a second?" he asked as he lightly grabbed my arm and walked me away from Claire.

"What's up?"

"I'm happy you and Christian are dating. I was worried there for a while that he would try and make a move on Claire."

I rolled my eyes at him.

"Can I give you a piece of advice, Kenny?"

"Sure."

"Stop this jealousy thing you have going on. Claire loves you

223

to death and I've never seen her happier. But everyone has their limits, and if you keep this up, you're going to push her away and into the arms of another man. I know your last girlfriend screwed you over, but don't let your past define who you are in the present. Trust is very important in a relationship and if you keep giving out that vibe of mistrust to her, you're going to lose her."

"I do trust her. It's the other men I don't trust."

"Come on, Kenny, we both know the truth. Because of what happened with your ex, you project all the women you date to be like that. Am I right?"

"I don't know." He looked down.

"Just think about what I said. I don't want to see the two of you split up over something that could have been prevented."

He gave me a small smile as he placed his hand on my arm.

"Thanks, Eloise."

"Excuse me?" Claire yelled. "If the two of you are finished, I would like to go eat. I'm starving!"

I glanced over at Claire and gave her a smile before heading to Christian's office. When I arrived, he was on the phone but motioned for me to come in. I set the photos on the table in his office and he hung up from his call and walked over to me.

"God, I missed you." He kissed my lips.

"I just saw you five hours ago." I laughed.

"Five hours is a long time, babe."

"You're right. It is." I kissed him.

#Delete

Joe cleared his throat as he stood in the doorway of Christian's office.

"If you two are finished with your PDA, I would like to see the photographs." He smiled. "I brought lunch for all of us. I had your secretary take it into the conference room."

I grabbed the photos from the table and the three of us walked down to the conference room. Christian gave me the honor of standing at the head of the table and pulling the photographs out of the envelope one by one. Joe loved them, and when I pulled out the black and white photo of the model naked in bed with the sheet barely covering her, he gasped.

"I would remember that shot," he spoke.

"I took it after you left. I had an idea and I went with it."

He got up from his seat, took the photo from my hand, and studied it.

"This is brilliant, Eloise. Do you have any others like this?"

"A few."

"Send them to Christian as soon as you can. I think I know what we can do with them. My God, you're a genius." He kissed my cheek. "I've been wanting to do a special test campaign for a long time but was afraid to put it in motion because of the other VP's. But this, this photo, her look, the expression on her face, it screams sensuality!" he exclaimed. "This is the vision I had."

"Thank you. I'm happy you like it."

"No, darling. I love it. Christian, I want to meet with you and your design team. Our one campaign just turned into two." He smiled. "I have a few errands to run. I'll be back around five o'clock for that meeting. Is that okay?"

"Five is fine," Christian replied.

"Great. Excellent work, Eloise. I will definitely be keeping your number handy." He winked.

Christian walked over and wrapped his arms around me.

"Thank you." He kissed the side of my head. "I knew I made the right decision hiring you for this job."

"Was my work the only reason?" I arched my brow at him.

"I'm not going to answer that question." He smirked.

I hooked my arm around his and we walked back to his office. He took his phone from his pocket and set it down on his desk.

"Dinner tonight at your place after my meeting with Ron?" He grinned as he placed his hands on each side of my face.

"Dinner or sex?" I asked with a raised brow.

"Both. You can't have one without the other." His lips softly brushed against mine.

"I agree. If you were only going to say 'dinner,' I would have declined, Mr. Blake."

"Is that so?" His lips touched mine once again.

"Uh huh." I smiled and our kiss deepened.

"Sorry to interrupt, Christian, but Jimmy asked if you could go look at something in the draft room real quick," his secretary spoke from the doorway.

#Delete

"Tell him I'll be there in a minute."

"Jimmy interrupted our kiss," I spoke.

"I'll only be a few minutes. If you wait for me, we can continue where we left off."

I gave him a smile as he walked out of his office. Sitting down in the chair across from his desk, I pulled my phone from my purse to see if I had any messages. I didn't. The last time I heard from Mobile Man was yesterday afternoon. This whole situation was bothering me and it needed to be addressed.

"Hi. I don't know what's going on and why you've practically stopped texting me. If you're busy, please just tell me. Don't start pulling this shit. Not with me of all people."

I hit the send button and Christian's phone dinged. I didn't think anything of it. I stared at my phone and waited for a reply. After five minutes passed, I sent him another text.

"I thought we were friends, Mobile Man. You're doing to me what a typical douchebag guy would do and I want to know what I did wrong."

I hit the send button and Christian's phone dinged again. I furrowed my brows as a sick feeling washed over me. "My god, Eloise, don't be stupid," I said to myself.

"Mobile Man?"

I hit the send button and Christian's phone dinged.

"Hello?"

Another ding.

"Hello?"

Another ding.

My heart started racing as I slowly got up from my chair and walked over to where his phone was sitting on his desk. With shaking hands, I picked it up and saw the name Digits appear on his lock screen. A violent wave of nausea overtook me and my legs began to shake. This couldn't be happening. Christian was Mobile Man? He walked into his office and stopped when he saw his phone in my hand.

"Eloise?"

"I don't know what to say, Christian," I spoke in shock.

"I'm so sorry. I wanted to tell you, but I didn't know how."

I stared blankly at him for a moment as silence overtook me. It took a few seconds for my brain to process what he'd just said.

"What?" I cocked my head as tears instantly filled my eyes. "You knew I was Digits and you didn't tell me?"

"Baby." He walked over to me.

"STOP!" I put my hand up to prevent him from coming any closer. "ANSWER MY QUESTION!" I shouted.

"Yes. I knew." He lowered his head.

The air around me constricted my lungs so tightly, I felt as if I couldn't breathe.

"How long have you known?" I asked in a shaky voice.

"I found out that night I came to your apartment to look at your work."

#*Delete*

"And you kept it from me? Why the fuck would you keep that from me?!"

"I wanted to tell you. I really did, and you have to believe me. I just didn't know how."

I swallowed hard as the tears flowed freely down my face.

"All this time. All those text messages. Text messages spilling my guts about you, telling you how I felt and you encouraging me to let my guard down and go for it! How could you do that to me? HOW!" I slammed my fist down on his desk.

"I don't know. I didn't want to hurt you. And you need to remember that in all those text messages, you, Eloise, YOU were the woman I was talking about." He pointed his finger at me.

"Oh my god, you used what I said to your advantage. Was this all a game to you?" I scowled at him.

"No. Of course not! How could you even think that?!" he growled.

"What were you going to do, Christian? Disappear as Mobile Man and pray I never found out?! Was that your plan?!"

"No."

"Really? Because you haven't texted me since yesterday afternoon!"

"I was pulling back." He shook his head. "Fuck, Eloise. I'm sorry. You have to believe that."

"Well, I don't!" I screamed.

"Everything I said to you in those text messages was the

goddamn truth!" he shouted. "Every single word!"

"Wow." I shook my head. "I just realized something. You didn't want to talk about your family because you already told me, and if you told me again, then I would know who Mobile Man was. Is that how you found out that night I was Digits? Because I told you about my parents?"

"Yes," he softly spoke. "Then when I told you I had to use the bathroom, I stood around the corner and texted you to confirm my suspicions."

I placed my hands on my head and paced around his office, tears still streaming down my face.

"Fuck!" I yelled.

"Eloise, please."

"Don't." I pointed my finger at him in anger. "Don't you say a word to me. You don't get to say anything! You betrayed me, Christian. You knew who I was and you didn't tell me."

"You're right, I didn't. Maybe if you weren't so fucking hell bent on not meeting Mobile Man, this never would have happened!"

"So it's my fault?" I yelled.

"What is going on?" Claire asked as she stood in the doorway. "I just got back from lunch and everyone can hear you!"

"We're done, Christian. Don't ever call or talk to me again." I grabbed my purse and began to head towards the door. Then suddenly I stopped and turned to him. "Wait a minute. You have two phone numbers? Because the number you gave me isn't the same as Mobile Man's. Wait. Don't answer that. If you would have given me your number, I would have known. So you got a second number so I wouldn't find out?"

He stared at me from across the room and didn't say a word. His silence told me everything.

"Oh my god. I don't ever want to see you again." I stormed out of his office, practically knocking Claire down on my way out.

Chapter Thirty-Six

Christian

"Eloise, wait!" I shouted as I began to go after her.

"No, Christian. Let her go," Claire firmly spoke as she stopped me. "She's in shock. Let her go."

I walked over to my desk, and in a fit of rage, I swiped my hand across it, knocking everything except my computer off.

"Why did you pick here in the office to tell her?" Claire asked.

"I didn't. Apparently, she was texting Mobile Man and my phone was sitting on the desk. I was with Jimmy looking over some prints."

"Wait a minute. Then there was no way she knew you knew."

"No shit. I'm thinking that now. But at the time when I walked in and saw her standing there with my phone in her hand, the only thing I could say was that I wanted to tell her."

"YOU IDIOT! You could have acted like you didn't know and you both found out together at the same time!"

"I realized that after I told her I was sorry. I'm so stupid." I sat down in my chair and placed my face in my hands.

#Delete

"We'll talk about this later. I need to go after her."

I needed to get out of here. Grabbing my briefcase, I left my office and told my secretary that I wouldn't be back for the rest of the day. FUCK! I forgot about my meeting with Ron. After hailing a cab back to my apartment, I sent a group text message to my design team and told them to be at my house promptly at five o'clock for a meeting. Then, I sent a text message to Ron.

"We'll need to meet at my apartment for the meeting if that's okay? Something's come up and I had to leave the office."

"Sure, Christian. Your place is fine. Text me the address."

****

Eloise

"Eloise, wait," Claire shouted as I walked down the street.

"Claire, please leave me alone. I don't want to talk to anyone right now. Please."

She caught up with me and lightly grabbed hold of my arm.

"What happened between you and Christian?"

"I can't talk about it. Not now. Please, just give me some time." The tears continued to fall.

"Okay. But please call me later."

I gave her a slight nod and continued walking down the street and around the block. Where was I going? I thought home, but home was too far to walk. So I was just walking to nowhere. After wandering around the streets of New York with tears streaming down my face and the sympathetic looks from strangers, I hailed a cab back to my apartment.

I needed to calm down. My mind was racing a mile a minute and I couldn't keep up with it. I was drained, both mentally and physically. I took a glass down and poured some wine into it. Bringing the red liquid up to my lips, I gulped it as if it were water. I could feel the alcohol soothing my nerves as it flowed through my body. Picking up the bottle, I poured another glass, took it over to the couch, and wrapped myself in my soft gray blanket. I could hear the annoying dings of text messages coming through to my phone, but I didn't care. I wasn't about to get up and see whom they were from. I slowly sipped on my wine as I thought about Christian. How could he do this to me? Of all men, I thought he was different. He was the rare find I'd been searching for my entire life. All those text messages from him encouraging me to go out with him. All those things he said about waking up one day and wondering what could have been. I felt sick to my stomach and I jumped off the couch and ran to the bathroom, where I vomited in the toilet. When I was done, I started the water for a bath. After grabbing a bath bomb and putting it in the water, I climbed in and laid back, closing my eyes and trying to escape the shit show of today.

My heart was completely shattered. I'd had many broken hearts in my lifetime, but never shattered. I couldn't comprehend his reasoning for not telling me. Or maybe I could. It was all a game to him. He wanted to take me out and I rejected him. He knew I didn't want to date, and when he found out I was Digits, the girl who sent him that nasty text message by mistake, he took advantage of it for his own sake and to get what he wanted. Tears started to fall down my face again and I lay in the tub and cried my shattered heart out.

****

Christian

#Delete

I sat there, staring into space as Ron shared his vision with my design team. I hurt so bad. A hurt I'd never felt before. Not even with my ex-girlfriends. My life fell apart in a matter of seconds, and over what? Some fucking text messages. I knew what I did was wrong and I'd struggled with the decision of telling her since I'd found out. I could sit here all fucking night and analyze the what if's. But it wouldn't change anything. The damage was done. I was done. Eloise made it very clear she never wanted to see or talk to me again. I couldn't accept that. I needed her in my life. I wanted her in my life.

"Earth to Christian," Ron spoke.

Snapping back into the dark reality, I looked over at him.

"Sorry. I have a lot on my mind."

"I think we're finished here." He smiled.

"Sorry I had to have the meeting here. Something came up and I wouldn't have gotten back to the office on time."

"It's not a problem. Everything okay?" he asked. "You're not having problems with Eloise, are you?"

"We got into a huge fight earlier."

He patted me on the back as he walked to the door.

"Couples fight all the time. You two will figure it out," he spoke.

"Thanks, Ron. I'll give you a call when the campaign is ready."

"Sounds good. Take care, Christian."

"You too."

I shut the door and poured myself a whisky, something I rarely drank, but today it was warranted. I did a couple shots, poured a full glass, and sat down on the couch to drink my troubles away. How was I going to fix this? I guess meeting her parents on Saturday was out of the question, not to mention the Broadway tickets I'd bought for Sunday evening.

"FUCK!" I yelled as I threw my glass at the wall.

#Delete

Chapter Thirty-Seven

Eloise

The moment I stepped out of the tub and changed into my pajamas, there was a knock at the door.

"Eloise, it's us. Open up!" Natalie shouted.

Rolling my eyes and mad as hell that they couldn't respect my wishes, I reluctantly opened the door and all three of them stood there with pouts on their faces.

"We're your best friends and we're here for you," Natalie spoke as she pushed me aside and walked in.

"We brought pizza," Claire spoke.

"And ice cream." Scarlett smiled.

"I appreciate it, you guys, but—"

"No buts," Natalie spoke. "When you're hurting, we're hurting. That's how it's always been."

Scarlett placed her arm around my shoulders and led me over to the couch.

"You go sit down and get comfortable. We'll bring the food over."

"And then you're going to tell us what the fuck happened with Christian," Natalie spoke.

Claire brought the paper plates, napkins, and the box of pizza over to the coffee table. After placing a piece on a plate, she handed it to me.

"I'm not hungry."

"We don't care," she spoke. "You know the tradition. When one of us is upset, we all eat comfort food together."

"Tell us what happened," Scarlett spoke.

"You're never going to believe it. So brace yourselves. Christian Blake is Mobile Man."

"Shut the fuck up!" Natalie exclaimed.

"Oh my god, Eloise," Claire spoke.

"I'm sorry. What?" Scarlett asked.

I explained to them the whole story and they sat there in complete shock.

"I have no words for what you just told us," Scarlett spoke.

"I'm sorry, Eloise." Natalie hooked her arm around me and pulled me into her, which made me cry even harder.

"I'm sorry," Claire spoke. "I can't believe Christian would do something like that."

"Well, believe it," I spoke with a hint of anger. "He's an asshole like the rest of them."

"Eloise, I know you're in shock over this, but just try to think rationally for a minute. Yes, he knew you were Digits and he

#Delete

didn't tell you. But you knew Mobile Man before him and you connected with him instantly. Then you met Christian and you connected with him almost instantly. The same person. Doesn't that say something?" Claire asked.

"He used knowing that I was Digits to his advantage! He pushed me to go out with him. To give him a chance. I will never forgive him for that. He deceived me and that is something I will not put up with."

We talked until about one a.m. and the girls decided it was time to leave.

"Try and get some sleep. We'll call you tomorrow," Claire spoke.

"Thanks for being pushy." I managed a smile.

"That's what sister friends are for, baby." Natalie hugged me tight.

After they left and I locked up, I climbed into bed and tried to get comfortable. I lay there and stared at the side that was still made up where he'd lay with me at night. Even though we hadn't spent many nights together, it felt like it had been years. I fell for him and I fell fast. Just like I knew I would the moment I met him. I closed my eyes and finally drifted off into a deep sleep.

I struggled to open my swollen eyes, and when I did, it was daylight. When I rolled over and looked at my clock on the nightstand, it read two thirty. My head was pounding and my eyes hurt too much to keep them open, so instead, I gave in and went back to sleep. I didn't care what was going on in the outside world. All I wanted to do was sleep and forget about everything and everyone.

Sandi Lynn

****

Christian

I stumbled into the office around twelve thirty, and when I walked past Claire's cubicle, she looked at me.

"You look like shit," she spoke.

"I feel like shit, and don't forget I'm still your boss."

I walked into my office and she followed behind me with a cup of coffee.

"Here," she spoke.

"Thanks."

I sat down at my desk and immediately took out the bottle of aspirin from the top drawer.

"How is she?" I asked.

"How do you think, Christian? She's broken, devastated, and a mess. We were at her apartment last night until one a.m. trying to comfort her because she couldn't stop crying."

I sighed.

"I sent her a couple of text messages, but she didn't respond," I spoke.

"You really thought she'd respond to you? She probably already #Deleted your dumb ass. And she probably blocked your number as well. I've been with her through many heartbreaks and I've never seen her like she was last night."

"I'm sorry, Claire. I really am. I'm in love with her and I won't accept never seeing her again."

#Delete

"Well, I don't know what you're going to do. All she kept saying last night was how you betrayed and deceived her. You're just going to have to give her some time to calm down. Maybe once she does and she clears her head, she'll be able to think more clearly and be open to talking to you about it."

"Thanks, Claire. I'm sure your other friends hate me."

"They do." She smiled. "I sort of stuck up for you, but Eloise wasn't having it."

"I appreciate it. But I don't want you to get involved. The last thing I need is for her getting mad at you."

"I've got to get back to work."

"Thank you for the coffee and the chat."

"You're welcome." She smiled as she walked out of my office.

Sandi Lynn

Chapter Thirty-Eight

Eloise

It was six o'clock p.m. when I finally climbed out of bed. Walking into the bathroom, I splashed my face with some cold water and looked at my dreaded self in the mirror. My eyes were still puffy and red and I had blotches all over my face. My body ached and it was a struggle to even walk to the kitchen to make a cup of coffee. While the coffee was brewing, I pulled my phone from my purse and saw I had two missed calls from Natalie, three missed calls from Scarlett, one missed call from Claire, a dozen text messages from all three of them, and two messages from Christian. Like an idiot, I opened the messages from Christian first.

"Eloise, please talk to me. I'm so sorry for everything. We need to talk this out."

"I know I've hurt you and I can't say sorry enough. I'm begging you to please talk to me. The last week we spent together was the best week of my life. You're the best thing that has ever happened to me. Please, baby. Please just talk to me."

I sent text messages back to the girls telling them that I was okay and that I was going to shut my phone off for the rest of the night and do some work. I needed to keep myself occupied, but I didn't want to go out. Opening my emails, I sat there sipping my coffee and reading the compliments I had received

#Delete

from women all over the world who were using the #Delete method. I could sense the excitement in their words and how my videos and blog posts had helped them so much. I started reading over some of my older blog posts and came across one I had forgotten about. It was a post about not allowing yourself to wallow in self-pity and hurt for more than twenty-four hours after a breakup. I read it as if someone else had written it.

Who was I? Who the hell was I to give out this advice if I wasn't going to take it myself? I felt like a fraud as I sat there feeling sorry for myself in such a devastated state. The pain hadn't lessened, but I knew I had to get myself back on track, no matter how hard it would be. So I put on some makeup, fixed my hair, and filmed a video on how to deal with a breakup and what you should do to help yourself heal.

After I was done filming, I decided to wait and edit the video tomorrow morning. I thought about cancelling dinner with my parents because I dreaded telling them what happened between me and Christian. But staying home and feeling sorry for myself wasn't an option. Plus, I hadn't seen them in a while, and right now, I needed my mom. Looking over Christian's text messages again, I decided to respond. Not for him, but for my peace of mind. It felt weird texting him as Christian at the number I'd only known as Mobile Man's.

"You're sorry. I get that. But I can't be in a relationship with someone who deceived me. Even after what transpired yesterday, I still like you, but I don't need you. I was fine before you walked into my life and I'll be fine now that you're gone and no longer in it."

I hit the send button and threw my phone down. I expected a response ASAP, but as the night went on, a response never came. I'd said my peace in a nice way. I could have gone off on him and called him every name in the book because God knows he deserved it, but I couldn't. The intense pain I felt inside was disappointment. Disappointment in the fact that Christian didn't turn out to be who I thought he was or who I wanted him to be.

****

Christian

Her text message to me was brutally heartbreaking. To be honest, I expected a lot worse. At least she didn't tell me that she hated me. She still liked me, but she didn't need me and those words right there caused a lump in my throat that nearly suffocated me. I needed to respond, but I didn't know what to say. So I didn't. I said what I needed to in my last two text messages and she said what she needed to in hers. But just because she didn't need me didn't mean that I was going to stop trying. Eloise and I belonged together. I made one stupid mistake and I would spend the rest of my life figuring out how to make it up to her. She may have thought she didn't need me, but she did. She needed me to love her, to be there for her when she was having a bad day, and to support her in everything she did.

****

Eloise

The next morning, I climbed out of bed at six a.m. and headed to the gym. It wasn't a place I went to every day, but on occasion when I felt like I needed to get back into my self-love practices, I would go. The pain in my heart was still heavy, but I was going to practice what I preached. I allowed myself twenty-four hours of depression and wallowing in self-pity and that was long enough. I needed to get back to my life before Christian stepped into it, and I was determined to get through

#Delete

this, no matter what it took.

I put my headphones on and climbed on the treadmill. As I was running and looking out the window at the people passing by on the street, I saw Christian walk in. What the fuck? Was he stalking me or something? An unsettling nervousness took over me. There was no way he could see me. I was at the opposite end of the door, second row, sandwiched between two other people. I watched as he checked in and stared straight ahead as he walked to the locker room. I let out the deep breath I was holding and continued to run. He lifted weights, so I was positive he would go to the weight area and then I wouldn't have to see him. The girl that was next to me climbed off and it was the only treadmill open. My heart started rapidly pounding as thoughts of him getting on next me infiltrated my head. I stared straight ahead, and as I listened to my music, I silently prayed.

Crisis averted. I ran on the treadmill for forty-five minutes and then I needed to get home and edit my video so I could upload it. I turned off my music, took my headphones off, and headed to the locker room, praying all the way he wouldn't see me.

"Hey, Eloise, wait up!" I heard a man's voice speak.

I turned around and it was Curtis, one of the models I shot for a magazine spread.

"Curtis, hey. How are you?" I nervously spoke because I didn't want to stop and talk. But I couldn't be rude.

"I'm good. How are you? You're an early bird this morning." He grinned.

"Yeah. Thought I'd come in and do some cardio before

starting the day."

"It was good to see you. Have a great day!"

"You too, Curtis."

Just as I turned around to go to the locker room, I ran right into Christian. Our eyes locked and the tension between us was noticeable.

"Eloise," he softly spoke.

"I didn't know you came to this gym," I spoke.

"I usually go to the other one by my apartment, but they didn't have any power this morning, so I came here. I didn't know you came here."

"I do sometimes." I swallowed hard as he stood before me, a sweaty, sexy mess.

"Weird how we both seem to be here this morning," he spoke.

"I need to go. I have things to do." I began to walk away, when he called out my name.

"Eloise?"

I stopped but didn't turn around.

"I'm sorry for everything. The last thing I ever wanted to do was hurt you."

I continued walking to the locker room, and when I reached it, I sat down on the bench and tried to hold back the tears that were forcing their way out. I grabbed my stuff and got out of there as fast as I could, went home, edited my video, and

#Delete

uploaded it.

Chapter Thirty-Nine

Two Weeks Later

Eloise

I kept myself busy by making videos, picking up a couple of photography jobs, and going out with my girls. Today was Hannah's birthday party and I couldn't wait to give her the doll I'd bought her in Chicago. I took the lid off the box to put the pajama set I'd bought inside. I picked it up and a small smile crossed my lips as I remembered Christian was the one who picked it out. It was a smile with a tinge of sadness mixed in. One day I was completely fine, and the next, sadness crept in when I saw things that reminded me of him.

My father sat down and had a talk with me that day I went to my parents' house. He asked me if I made a list of pros and cons, and to be honest, I didn't. I had in the past with other guys, but for some reason, it didn't cross my mind with Christian. He handed me a piece of paper and a pen and I made the list in front of him. The results didn't surprise me. On the con side, there was only one thing listed; what he did to me, or should I say, what he kept from me. My father looked at me with a small smile and told me to think about that list because everybody is entitled to make a mistake at least once in their life.

I wrapped up the doll and headed over to Scarlett and Jeff's

#Delete

apartment. I was the first to arrive, which was no surprise to anyone since I always liked to be a little early.

"I'm so happy you're here." Scarlett smiled as she hugged me.

"Good to see you, Eloise. How are you?" Jeff asked as he lightly kissed my cheek.

"I'm okay."

"I have to tell you that I've been watching your YouTube channel. If I were a woman, I would totally be inspired by you." He smirked.

"Thanks, Jeff." I laughed.

"Listen, there's something I want to talk to you about."

"Sure, what is it?"

"A friend of mine is hosting a woman's personal growth seminar at the PlayStation Theater next weekend and she's trying to fill two spots where speakers have had to cancel. I was telling her about you and she watched one of your videos and she's highly impressed. She said she would love to have you as a guest speaker if you're interested. There will be approximately fifteen hundred women attending."

"Are you serious?" I asked in shock.

"Yes." He reached into his wallet and handed me her business card. "Her name is Talia Springwater. Give her a call. I think you'd be great."

"I don't know, Jeff. I've never spoken in front of a live audience before."

"You speak to millions of people all over the world every day!" Scarlett chimed in.

"That's different. I'm behind a camera. I don't actually see the people."

"I think you should do it. It'll be good for you." She smiled.

I thanked Jeff and put Talia's business card in my purse. Everyone had started to trickle in and the party began. I sat with Claire and Natalie, and as we ate, I asked their thoughts about participating in Talia's seminar.

"I think it's a great idea. You'd be a fool to turn it down," Claire spoke.

"This is what you're passionate about. Plus, you never know what other doors this opportunity could open." Natalie smiled.

"By the way, where's Nathan? I thought he was coming."

"So did I, but something came up and he had to cancel." Natalie frowned. "I think the time has come to #Delete him. I'm not playing this cat and mouse game with him. Me being the cat and chasing him. Like you say, he's giving low investment. Do you know that he didn't text or call me for two days?"

"What was his excuse?" I asked.

"He was overwhelmed with work." She rolled her eyes.

"I still think he has a girlfriend," Claire spoke.

"I'm sorry, Natalie, but I have to agree."

"Yeah. My gut is telling me the same thing. I didn't want to believe it at first, but things are starting to point in that direction."

#Delete

Scarlett helped Hannah open her gifts and when she got to mine, Hannah ripped the baby from the box and hugged her tight.

"Oh my god, Eloise, I love this," Scarlett spoke as she held up the pajamas.

Tears started to fill my eyes. Damn it!

"What's wrong?" Natalie asked as she put her arm around me.

"Nothing. It's just look at how much Hannah loves her doll," I spoke as I lightly wiped my eye. "It kind of reminds me of when I got my first American Girl doll, Maggie."

That wasn't the reason at all. The reason was those damn pajamas reminded me of Christian and the time we spent together in Chicago.

"You bought that doll in Chicago. Are you sure there isn't another reason why you're all teary eyed?" Natalie asked.

"No. There isn't," I lied.

"Come here, you little liar." She pulled me into her. "I thought you were doing better."

"I am. At least ninety percent of the time. Chicago was one of the best times of my life and the memory will always be there. So it's okay to get a little sad thinking about it every once in a while knowing that I won't experience that again."

"You could always give a call or shoot him a text," Claire spoke.

"Why would I do that? Anyway, I #Deleted him. So I don't even have his number or numbers anymore. Remember, he got a second one so I wouldn't know he was Mobile Man." I narrowed my eye. "I don't want to talk about Christian anymore. Let's go have some cake." I smiled.

#Delete

Chapter Forty

Eloise

The next morning, after being up all night thinking, I pulled Talia's business card from my purse and gave her a call.

"Talia Springwater," she answered.

"Hi, Talia. My name is Eloise Moore and a mutual friend of ours, Jeff Woodsbury, said that you were interested in me being a guest speaker for your seminar next weekend."

"Ah, yes. Eloise. I'm so happy you called. I would love to have you as a guest speaker. I've researched your blog and I've watched your YouTube channel. I must say, you really caught my attention with your #Delete concept. My seminar is about empowering women in every aspect of their life and personal growth, and I think your talk about #Delete and guys behaving badly would fit in perfectly. I think too many women sit around and waste their time with a guy who isn't serious about them. Lord knows I've done it many times."

"Thank you, Talia. After giving it some thought, I'd love to be a guest speaker."

"Excellent! Are you available for lunch tomorrow afternoon at Bryant Park Grill, say around twelve thirty?" I'd love to meet you first and tell you a little bit about my seminars."

"Twelve thirty would be great. I'll see you there."

"Thank you, Eloise, for getting in touch. I look forward to meeting you."

I ended the call and sat there for a moment while I sipped my coffee. I was startled by a knock on my door. Getting up from the table, I looked out the peep hole and asked who it was.

"I have a delivery for Miss Eloise Moore," the young man spoke.

I opened the door and he handed me a large envelope marked "fragile."

"Thank you." I smiled as I shut the door.

I noticed the return address was from Christian's firm, Blake Group. Opening the envelope, I pulled out three large Chanel campaign photos with a note from Christian.

Here are the final photos for the Chanel campaign. I thought you'd like to have a copy of each for your portfolio. The people over at Chanel loved them and are very pleased. Thank you again for being a part of the campaign. This wouldn't have been possible without you.

Christian Blake

I stared at his name for a moment until the sudden ring of my phone startled me. Picking it up, I saw it was Natalie calling.

"Hello," I answered.

"I just found out Nathan has a girlfriend that he's been living with for about six months."

"How did you find out?"

#Delete

"A couple came in and wanted to hire me for their son's birthday party. We got to talking and she mentioned her brother was an architect. I asked her his name and she said Nathan."

"Do you know how many people in New York have siblings named Nathan?"

"Who lives on Long Island and just went on a business trip to Hawaii that he can't stop talking about?"

"Oh. I'm sorry, Natalie."

"Me too. But you said right from the start something was off. I should have listened to you after he cancelled our second and third date at the last minute."

"You know what to do, right?" I asked.

"Already done, sista!"

"Do you need some friend time?"

"Nah. I'm okay. Just another douchebag to toss into the sea."

I let out a light laugh. "The sea is going to be overfilled with them shortly."

"I'll talk to you later, Eloise. I have a client meeting in ten."

"Okay. Bye."

I continued looking at the photos and thought that maybe I should send Christian a text message thanking him for sending them over. He could have brought them himself, but he didn't because he knew I wouldn't want to see him. I respected him for that. It was obvious to me that he was already over our breakup. It didn't surprise me, though; men usually recovered quicker than women did.

It was the middle of the afternoon, and after I finished filming another video, I decided to take my laptop to Starbucks, order a coffee, and edit my video there. I needed to get out of this apartment. As I was editing, I happened to look up and see Christian standing in line. Instantly, my heart started racing. What was he doing here in the middle of the afternoon? He didn't see me, but then again, he wasn't looking around. He ordered his drink and stood in the pickup line while it was being made. This was my opportunity to thank him for the photos since I couldn't text him. But did I want to? Texting him was one thing, but doing it in person was another. He grabbed his coffee from the counter and started heading towards the door. I wrestled with the do I or don't I. The do I won.

"Christian," I yelled.

He turned his head and looked at me. He stood still for a moment and then made his way over to my table.

"Hello, Eloise."

"Hi. I'm happy I saw you here. I got the photos you sent over this morning. Thank you."

"You're welcome. I thought it would be a nice addition to your portfolio." He lightly smiled.

Now the awkwardness set in. Neither one of us knew what to say to each other.

"So what are you doing here in the middle of the afternoon?" I asked.

"I had a meeting not too far from here. I'm heading back to the office now. Are you working?" He pointed to my laptop.

"Yeah. I'm editing a video."

#Delete

"Cool. Well, it was good to see you. Enjoy the rest of your day."

"Thanks. You too. Hey, Christian?" I spoke as he began to walk away.

"Yeah?"

"I'm going to be a guest speaker for Talia Springwater's seminar at the PlayStation Theater next weekend."

"Really? I've heard of her. Wow. That's great, Eloise. Congratulations." He smiled.

"Thank you. I'm really nervous. I've never spoken in front of a large crowd like that before."

"You'll do fine." He winked. "I have to get going."

"Okay. Catch ya later?" Those damn words just fell out of my mouth and I wanted to die a thousand times over. What the fuck?

He stared at me for a moment and his eyes burned into mine.

"Catch ya later." He smirked.

After he left, I brought my hand to my forehead and pounded on it.

"You idiot!" I whispered to myself. "What the hell were you thinking?"

Chapter Forty-One

Christian

I walked out of Starbucks with a smile on my face. I was surprised she called me over, which, to me, was a good start. I had been watching her YouTube videos and missing her more and more every day. I needed to prove to her that we were meant to be together and that I could be the man she'd been searching for her entire life.

When I arrived back to the firm, I called Claire into my office.

"What's up, Christian?" she asked as she took a seat across from me.

"I just ran into Eloise over at Starbucks."

"Oh? And how did that go? Or don't I want to know?"

"She was sitting at a table and called me over."

"What? Seriously?"

"She thanked me for the Chanel photos I sent her this morning."

"Oh yeah. She probably would have sent you a text message, but you've been #Deleted."

#Delete

"I figured as much." I sighed. "Anyway, she told me she was going to be a guest speaker next weekend for Talia Springwater."

"Oh good, she is doing it. Natalie and I told her she'd be crazy not to. So, she was civil to you?"

"Yes. Very much so. I've ordered her something and it should be arriving to her apartment in a couple of days."

"What did you order her?" She smiled.

"I'm not going to say. You'll just have to wait and see."

"Oh, come on, Christian."

"I'm sure she'll be calling you once she gets it."

"Fine." She huffed. "But why did you order her something?"

"Because I know she'll love it and I want to make her smile again."

Chapter Forty-Two

Eloise

A couple of days had passed and my lunch with Talia went well. I expressed to her my anxiety and nervousness about speaking in front of a large group. She laughed and told me everyone gets like that their first time on stage. She gave me some tips and told me just to go with the flow and let the lecture happen naturally.

I was sitting on the couch with my laptop making a couple of PowerPoints for the weekend, when there was a knock at my door. I looked through the peep hole and saw it was the UPS guy holding a large box in his hands. When I opened the door, he looked at the package and then at me.

"Are you Eloise Moore?" he asked.

"Yes, I am."

"This is for you and I'll need a signature."

He handed me the box and I signed for it.

"Thank you." I smiled.

"Have a nice day." He tipped his hat.

I had no idea what this could be because I hadn't ordered

#Delete

anything in a while. I took the scissors from the kitchen drawer and slid it down the box. Lifting the flaps, I stared at the large red box that had American Girl written across it and the white envelope that contained a card inside taped to it. After removing the envelope, I took the card out that said American Girl in gold across it and opened it.

Eloise,

The time we spent together was magical and a time I will never forget. I hurt you in a bad way and I'm truly sorry. I know how much Maggie meant to you and how the loss of her was devastating. I wanted you to have someone you can tell your deepest secrets to when you feel like you can't tell anyone else. I hope this doesn't upset you. That isn't my intention. I know you'll take good care of her and give her the home she deserves. She was made special for you.

Love, Christian

A single tear fell from my eye as I read his note. Removing the lid from the box, I cupped my mouth in my hand and began to cry as I looked at the American Girl doll that looked just like me; long brown hair with curls at the end and emerald green eyes. I didn't know what to think because I couldn't. My head was in a tizzy and millions of thoughts were running through my head at the same time. I removed the doll from the box and held her tight. Wiping my eyes, I took her over to the couch and sat down. She wore a white dress with small pink roses all over it, a plum sash around the waist, and a light blue denim jacket. I smiled when I looked down at her plum-colored Mary Jane style shoes. But the one thing that really choked me up was the little camera she held in her hand. Once I composed myself, I sent a group message to the girls.

"I really need you all to come over tonight for dinner. Six

o'clock. Scarlett, bring Hannah if Jeff won't be home."

A few moments later, all three of them replied that they would be here. As I stared at the doll, I knew I needed to name her. She looked just like Maggie and I didn't see any harm in naming her that. After all, some people named their new cats and dogs after the ones who passed away.

"Welcome home, Maggie." I smiled.

I finished my PowerPoint with Maggie by my side and placed a delivery order for Chinese, ordering everyone's favorite dish. When six o'clock rolled around, there was a knock at my door and Natalie, Scarlett, and Claire stood on the other side.

"Is everything okay?" Natalie asked as she hugged me.

"I think so."

"What do you mean?" Scarlett asked.

"Where's Hannah?"

"My mom came over and took her for the night."

"Is there a reason for this last-minute dinner get together?" Claire asked as all three of them followed me into the kitchen.

"What the fuck is that?" Natalie asked as she looked at Maggie. "That doll looks just like you."

"Oh my God. You bought an American Girl doll!" Scarlett exclaimed as she picked her up.

"I didn't buy her," I spoke. "She arrived today."

I picked up Christian's note and handed it to her while

#*Delete*

Natalie and Claire read it over her shoulder. A tear fell from Scarlett's eye as the other two tried to hold theirs back.

"This man is not #Delete worthy," Natalie spoke as she wiped her eye.

"I can't even believe he did that," Claire spoke.

"If you don't marry him, I will!" Scarlett said. "That has to be the sweetest thing in the world."

I couldn't help but let out a light laugh. "You're married."

"I'll divorce Jeff." She smiled.

Natalie walked over to me and hugged me tight. Then the other two joined us.

"You need to rethink everything, Eloise," Claire spoke.

"I agree. He's not a typical douchebag guy. He made a mistake and I think he's more than enough made it up to you."

"What did he say when you thanked him?" Claire asked.

"I haven't yet. I don't have his number, remember?"

"Then I think you should do it in person." She smiled.

"She's right, Eloise," Scarlett spoke.

"Yeah. This is a thank you that is in person worthy," Natalie spoke.

"Okay. I'll stop by the office tomorrow."

"He'll be there all day. He doesn't have any meetings scheduled," Claire spoke. "Plus, I'll be there if you need support."

After we ate, talked, and drank a bottle of wine between the four of us, I changed into my pajamas, sat Maggie on my dresser, and climbed into bed. I lay there thinking about tomorrow and what I wanted to say to him. My dad was right, everyone is entitled to make a mistake in their life. It's how we learn and grow as human beings. My father also pointed out that he wasn't the perfect man I saw him as, and if we truly cared for someone, we'd accept their flaws. Christian wasn't a man who consistently behaved badly. He did what he did because he was afraid of what my reaction would be and losing me. I'd done things before I wasn't proud of out of fear. I told him that I liked him, but I didn't need him. That still rang true. I didn't need him to be in my life, I wanted him to be.

#Delete

Chapter Forty-Three

Eloise

I took in a deep breath as I stepped into the elevator and took it up to the Blake Group. When I stepped out, I went to Christian's office and he wasn't in there.

"Can I help you?" his secretary asked.

"I'm looking for Christian. Is he around?"

"He just stepped out. He should be back shortly."

"Thank you. Is it okay if I wait in his office?"

"Of course." She smiled.

I took the seat across from his desk, and a few moments later, he walked in.

"Eloise?"

"Hi, Christian." I got up from my seat.

"What are you doing here?"

My nerves were getting the better part of me and I found it difficult to speak.

"I just wanted to come and thank you in person for the doll. She arrived yesterday."

"You're welcome." He smiled as he stood in front of me. "I hope you like her."

"I do. I love her." I smiled.

"What's her name?" He smirked.

"I named her Maggie."

"I figured you would." He grinned.

"Listen, Christian. I just want you to know that I forgive you, and maybe—"

"I know you do, Eloise, and I think I know what you're going to say. I didn't send you the doll with the hopes of getting back together. It was a small gesture to help heal the wound that I caused. I think maybe we're better off with the way things are."

I stood there in shock as my partially healed heart broke once again.

"Yeah. Maybe you're right." I looked down. "Thank you again," I spoke as I couldn't get out of there fast enough before the tears started to fall.

"You're welcome. I'll see you around."

"Sure." I gave a small smile to deflect the hurt I was feeling inside.

****

Natalie, Scarlett, and Claire dragged me out to Hellcat Annie's. I didn't want to go. All I wanted to do was curl up in bed and sleep the rest of the day and night away. But they weren't having it. As soon as we were seated, I ordered a

#Delete

cosmopolitan while we looked over the menu. I wasn't hungry because my stomach was nothing but a tightly twisted knot of sorrow and despair. The three of them talked while I pretended to listen.

"Cheer up, buttercup," Natalie spoke as she placed her hand on mine.

"Yeah. We're here to have fun tonight with lots of alcohol and comfort food," Scarlett spoke.

As I finished off my drink, I held my finger up to get our waiter's attention. I needed another drink ASAP.

"Excuse me. I'm headed over to the bar. What can I get you?" Christian asked as he pointed to my empty glass.

I stared at him as a smile crossed his face.

"A cosmopolitan."

"One cosmopolitan coming right up." He winked.

I looked over at the girls and they sat there smiling at me. I didn't know what the hell was going on, and between seeing Christian and the alcohol, my heart was beating at a rapid pace.

"We have to use the bathroom," Claire spoke as all three of them got up from their seats.

A few moments later, Christian walked over and set my drink down on the table.

"Thank you," I spoke.

"You're welcome. I'm Christian Blake." He extended his hand.

I stared at him for a moment with a narrowed eye.

"Eloise Moore." I placed my hand in his.

"It's nice to meet you, Eloise. Would you mind if I took a seat?"

"No. I wouldn't mind at all."

"Have you eaten yet?" he asked.

"I couldn't decide what to get," I nervously spoke.

"Their pulled pork sliders are the best. Have you tried them?"

"No. I haven't. But I think I would like to." A small smile crossed my lips.

Our waiter walked over and asked if we were ready to order.

"We'll both have the pulled pork sliders with fries," Christian spoke.

"We have three other people sitting with us. They just went to the restroom," I spoke to the waiter.

"Actually," Natalie spoke, "we need to get going. So you two enjoy the rest of your evening." She smiled.

I looked at them suspiciously as they said goodbye and left the restaurant.

****

Christian

With Claire's help, I had this all planned. I wanted to start over from the beginning. Just the two of us, Christian and

#Delete

Eloise. No Mobile Man and no Digits. I asked her about her career, she asked about mine, and we talked about our families. I told her everything about my parents and my childhood. We sat for four hours and just got to know each other again. It was after midnight when we finished off dessert and our last drink.

We left the restaurant and stood on the brightly lit street of 10th Avenue where I hailed her a cab home.

"I had a nice time, Eloise. I would love to see you again." I smiled.

"I would love to see you too." She smiled brightly back at me.

"Can I get your phone number?"

"Of course. I'd love for you have it."

She rattled off her number and I pretended to put it in my phone because I already had it. I quickly sent her a text message.

"I've sent you a text message so you have mine now." I smirked.

I opened the door to the cab and she climbed in.

"Catch ya later?" I asked with a grin.

"Catch ya later." The corners of her mouth curved up into a flirty smile.

For the next few days, we flirted via text and then we started seeing each other almost every night. I didn't dare make a move on her, even though it killed me not to. I wanted her in my bed more than anything in the world, but all good things come in time. I remembered her telling me that she never slept with a guy until after the fifth date, and I wanted to respect that, even though I knew she was getting restless. All was good and I would make sure it was worth the wait.

#Delete

Chapter Forty-Four

Eloise

I was sexually frustrated and he wasn't making a move, but I knew exactly why he was waiting. I had mentioned after we had sex the first time at his party that I didn't sleep with guys before the fifth date, and I was pretty sure he was waiting until then. I couldn't help but smile as I thought about it. He was the perfect gentleman, even though I didn't want him to be as far as sex was concerned. As for date nights, we took turns planning the date.

Our fifth date would be tomorrow night, Saturday night, after my speaking engagement, and I thought more about that than the lecture I was giving. It was my turn to plan the date and I had nothing but sex planned. The overwhelming feeling of happiness was back and my heart was whole once again.

Once word got out that I was going to be a guest speaker at the PlayStation Theater, six hundred more tickets were sold, placing the theater at full capacity. I couldn't wrap my head around everything that had happened so fast. It was as if #Delete made me an overnight sensation. Between the emails and messages, I found it hard to keep up, so I asked Scarlett if she would be my part-time assistant and she could work from home. She jumped at the chance in a second.

As I was going over my PowerPoint one last time, a text

message came through from Christian.

"Hello, gorgeous. I'll be by to pick you up at six o'clock for dinner."

"Hello, handsome. I'll be ready and waiting. Maybe we can come back to my place after for a drink." I sent the winky face.

"I actually made other plans for us for after dinner." He sent the smiley face.

"Oh? What are we doing?"

"You'll have to wait and find out."

"Are you being secretive?"

"Yes, I am. It's a surprise."

"I love surprises.

"I know you do. I'm heading to a meeting. Catch ya later, baby?"

"Catch ya later."

I smiled as I closed out of his message, gave my PowerPoint another look over, and then got ready for our date. Christian's planned date consisted of dinner at The Todd English Food Hall at the Plaza Hotel and then we were off to I didn't know where since he was keeping it a secret. After we finished eating, we walked out of the hotel, and sitting at the curb was a horse and carriage.

"Your ride awaits, Madame." Christian smiled as he held my hand.

"We're going on a horse and carriage ride?" I asked with

excitement.

"Yes, through Central Park."

With Christian's help, I climbed into the carriage and he climbed in next to me. The driver handed us a blanket since the chilly air had settled into the fall nights. Christian put his arm around me and as soon as I snuggled into him, he covered us with the warm blanket.

"This is beautiful. Thank you," I spoke.

"You're welcome." He kissed the top of my head.

It was a beautiful ride through Central Park, and when it was over, Christian took me home.

"I think you should come upstairs for a drink." I smiled as I took the lapels of his coat in my hands.

"We both know what will happen if I do." He smirked.

"And?" I raised my brow.

"You have a big day tomorrow and you need all the rest you can get."

I sighed.

"Hey." He placed his finger under my chin. "Tomorrow night is your turn to plan date night and we can do anything you want, and I mean anything." He winked.

A smile crossed my lips.

"Trust me. We will be."

He leaned in and brushed his lips against mine.

"Good night, Eloise." He stroked my cheek.

"Good night, Christian."

****

Christian

Saying good night to her on the doorstep of her building was hard. I wanted to come up to her apartment for a drink, but we both knew having a drink wasn't on either one of our minds. The past few nights being with her were difficult because all I wanted to do was take her to bed and never let her go. I could tell she was getting frustrated with me, but this was what needed to happen.

Tomorrow was a big day for her, and what she didn't know was that I'd bought a ticket, not only for myself, but for her friends as well. I didn't want to tell her because she'd be even more nervous than she already was. So, we'd just sit quietly in the way back and watch from afar.

#Delete

Chapter Forty-Five

Eloise

I stood behind the curtain, waiting for my turn. I was scheduled to go on stage in approximately five minutes. Was I ready? Fuck if I knew. The more I thought about it, the more anxiety set in. I'd made note cards like a school kid giving a presentation in front of the class. I stood there and studied them. Christian and I met for breakfast this morning and he gave me a pep talk. It helped. He always helped me. Even when he was Mobile Man, I instantly felt better after talking to him.

"You're on, Eloise!" Talia smiled. "Good luck."

"Thank you." I gave her a nervous smile.

My name was announced and I stepped on stage. I introduced myself, looked at my cards, and froze. Suddenly, my mind went blank and I couldn't comprehend what I had written down.

"Get hold of yourself!" I silently yelled in my head. "All these people want to hear what you have to say! Don't let them down!"

I stared at the massive crowd of women who sat proudly in their seats. Women who have, at least once in their lifetime, dealt with men behaving badly. I set my cards down on the chair at the end of the stage and then I took center and welcomed everyone in the theater as I started over.

"My name is Eloise Moore and I'm here to talk to you about a concept called #Delete. This concept applies to girls/women who are single and a part of the dating scene. I'm going to show you what to be on the lookout for when newly dating a guy. I'm going to teach you about the red flags, ghosting, benching, zombie-ing, breadcrumbing, and all the other signs of men behaving badly early on in dating. We as women spend far too much time and energy waiting for the guys we're interested in to text or call us, and then when they don't, we freak out, cry, wonder what's wrong with us, what did we do wrong, why don't they want us, how can I fix them, etc. The truth behind that is, it isn't us. *We* did nothing wrong. It could be as simple as the guy wasn't feeling it, which is okay. You're not going to mesh with everyone you meet.

But when a guy shows interest and behaves badly, then it's up to us to take action. That's where #Delete comes in. The moment he starts showing signs of all the millennial dating terms I previously spoke of, it's time to get rid of him and not play his games. Women today are too busy for games and we don't deserve to be treated like that. The most important thing I can't stress enough is for a woman to have standards. Once you know exactly what your standards are, you'll be able to spot the red flags instantly. For example, you meet a man and you both show interest in each other. You go on a couple of dates and then suddenly the text messages and the calls stop. No warning and no explanation. Two weeks go by since your last date and still nothing. That guy ghosted you, disappeared without a trace. You've been glued to your phone 24/7, staring at a black screen, hoping and praying he'll call. Your stomach is a nervous wreck and you keep replaying your last date over and over again, wondering what went wrong. You finally break down and send

#Delete

him a message. He doesn't respond. Your self-esteem is broken. Then a week later, he sends you a text, and you beam with excitement. Then you don't hear from him again. You try to pick yourself up, but you can't get him out of your mind, and why? The question you need to ask yourself is this: Am I really into him or is it the rejection that hurts me the most? Really stop and think about that. You'd only gone out with the guy a couple of times, sent a few dozen text messages, and maybe had a phone call or two. I can guarantee you that through all the nonsense you put yourself through over this one guy you barely knew, it was the rejection aspect of it.

It's very important that you, as a high valued woman who knows her self-worth and standards, give the same investment as the man you're trying to date does. If he's giving low investment into getting to know you better, you give low investment back. Nobody is ever too busy, and if a guy really likes you or wants to get to know you on a deeper level, he will make time to do it. I don't care if he's held up in meetings from nine to five. It takes as little as thirty seconds to type a message and hit send. Does he not go to the bathroom all day? Does he not get a lunch break? What about when he gets home from work? If a man can't take thirty seconds out of his busy day to say hi or that he's just thinking about you, then he's not thinking about you at all and it's time to #Delete and stop wasting your time. Same goes for a guy who takes three days to respond to your last text message. Is that really the kind of person you want to date? Now I'm not saying to #Delete him if he has an excuse and lets you know ahead of time, such as he's going camping and won't have reception or something. The important thing to remember is, if he ghosted you once, he'll do it again.

Now, let's talk about the guy who shows he is interested in you via text messaging but never actually takes you out or has any intention of actually getting serious. Let's say you've been talking to this guy for a week. You're getting to know each other and you're wondering why he hasn't asked you out yet. After all, he seems really into you. You make the bold move and ask him out for coffee or maybe for dinner. He makes an excuse as to why that weekend won't work for him. Another week goes by, and suddenly, the text messages become scarce. He's not texting you as much anymore. Your mind starts to go crazy. You talk about it with your friends. Your phone never leaves your sight just in case. Another week goes by, and out of the clear blue, he sends you a text saying 'Hey, what's up?' or 'Hey, how are you?' Instantly, you perk up and respond back to him immediately, which by the way, is one of the worst things you could do. You tell him how you're doing and how good it is to hear from him. You sit there and wait, watching your phone for a reply because he had just texted you a minute ago. But a reply doesn't come. You're devastated and the cycle starts all over again. He's doing what we like to call breadcrumbing. He may have been bored, feeling a little lonely or down and needed an ego boost. There are guys out there who like to keep a woman they've previously been talking to on the backburner for those instances, and by giving him an instant reply, you just showed him that no matter how sporadic or dick-like his messages are, you're still interested. Which leads me into the term 'benching.' He's not sure about you yet or someone else grabbed his attention while the two of you were still talking every day who he thought may be more interesting or a better fit for him. But instead of cutting you off completely, he sat you on the bench just in case he needs to come back to you some time in the future. He'll throw a text out there or maybe a phone call, just to make sure you're still interested. I like to call this emotional manipulation and it's not okay.

So what happens after you've been ghosted and then all of a

#Delete

sudden, a few months later, you get a text message from the guy asking what's up? Now, he's Zombie-ing you, or haunting you. Maybe the relationship he got into with the woman he ghosted you for wasn't working out, so he came across your number in his phone and thought he'd reach out because maybe you were still thinking about him. My advice, do not reply to the zombie at all! If he did it once, he'll do it again. Obviously, there was nothing there for him a few months ago when the two of you were talking, so why would there be now?

When do you #Delete a guy out of your life?

1. He doesn't respond to your text messages in a timely manner. If he waits five or six hours, that's not a good sign. Like I stated before, it only takes thirty seconds to type a text message and hit send. If you aren't worth thirty seconds of his time in a day, #Delete.
2. He asked you out, you went on a date, had a great time, and then he disappears. #Delete and don't give him another thought.
3. He's cancelled dates on you two or more times in a row. #Delete.
4. His text messages become scarce and you start receiving one here and there over a two- to three-week period. #Delete, especially when he doesn't offer an explanation for his lack of messaging.
5. He ghosted you, you #Delete him and then he returns a few months later as if nothing happened. Do not respond and #Delete again."

The guys who do these types of things aren't the guys for you and it's not the end of the world.

By accepting their behavior and stressing over why he hasn't called or texted, you're blocking the right person who was meant for you from coming into your life. I believe there is a special man out there for each and every one of us, and sometimes, we have to go through many douchebags in order to find our Prince Charming.

So, ladies, know your self-worth, set your standards, love yourself first, #Delete when necessary, and watch your life change. I promise you, it will."

The crowd applauded and stood from their seats. Tears filled my eyes as I took a bow and exited the stage.

"OH MY GOD! You were amazing!" Talia hugged me. "They loved you, Eloise."

"Thank you."

"You're a natural at this. I believe this is your calling."

"I don't know about that." I blushed.

"I think the standing ovation spoke for itself." She smiled.

#Delete

Chapter Forty-Six

Eloise

I walked to the lobby of the theater and was instantly greeted and congratulated by many women. The ones that bought tickets just to see me swarmed around, telling me how they've incorporated #Delete into their dating life and how much it had changed them. I felt like some sort of superstar, when really, I was just a girl who had gone through a lot of shit in her dating life. Many asked for pictures with me and I smiled with joy.

As I made my way through the crowd, I saw Christian, Natalie, Claire, and Scarlett standing by the doors.

"What are you guys doing here?" I asked as tears filled my eyes.

"Did you really think we'd miss this? Your debut stage appearance?" Natalie hugged me.

"You were amazing!" Claire excitedly spoke as she grabbed me from Natalie's arms and hugged me.

"I'm so proud of you, boss!" Scarlett smiled.

"Thank you."

"We're going to leave the two of you alone." Natalie grinned as she looked at Christian. "I'll call you tomorrow."

Christian wrapped his arms around me and kissed my lips.

"You were spectacular, baby. I am so damn proud of you."

"I didn't know you were here."

"I didn't want you to be any more nervous than you already were." He smirked. "Maybe this isn't the place to tell you, but I don't care because I need to say it right now, in this moment."

"Say what?" I cocked my head.

"I love you, Eloise. I am in love with you and I'm not going to stop loving you."

A wide grin crossed my face as my heart rapidly beat.

"I love you too, Christian."

His lips brushed against mine and then he looked at me.

"Didn't you say something about our date tonight being back at your place?"

"I sure did." I smiled. "I think we need to get back there now!"

"I couldn't agree more." He kissed my head.

The moment we entered my apartment, Christian scooped me up in his arms and carried me to the bedroom where we made love three times that night. And each time was just as magical as the first.

****

#Delete

Six Months Later

His finger dipped inside me and I gasped. Our mouths tangled with passion and I trembled at the touch of his hand on my breasts. I took down his pants with ease and released his throbbing hard cock in my hand. After a few strokes, he pushed everything on my overly cluttered table to the side and set me on it. He positioned his head in between my legs and explored every inch of my aching area with his tongue. I orgasmed and he smiled as he stood up and thrust inside me, my body taking in every inch of him. He moved in and out of me rapidly bringing me to the brink of another mind blowing orgasm. I yelled out his name as he halted deep inside and moaned while he released his excitement in me.

His lips pressed against mine and I smiled.

"I'm outgrowing this place."

He chuckled as he looked around the table at the mess that consumed it.

"Yes, you are. You need a place with an office."

"I know. I've been thinking about finding a new apartment."

"I'll help you look." He kissed my forehead and pulled out of me.

"I'd appreciate that." I grinned.

"I have a real estate guy. I'll give him a call tomorrow." Christian spoke as he handed me my clothes. "We need to be at my parents' house in fifteen minutes. I think we're going to be late."

I laughed. "Yeah. We can't get across town in fifteen

minutes. You might want to call them."

"And tell them what? We're going to be late because we just had sex on your dining room table?"

"Just tell them we're stuck in traffic." I smirked.

I loved Christian's parents and they loved me. My parents felt the same way about Christian and he and my dad started going on golf outings together. Even though photography was my first passion, I put my business on hold due to the success of my blog and YouTube channel. Things were moving in the right direction ever since I spoke at the PlayStation Theater. I ended up guest speaking a couple of more times for Talia and then I began booking seminars on my own, with the help of Scarlett, who was now my full-time assistant. A couple of months ago, I began writing a book and called it #Delete, which was contracted by Grand Central Publishing.

Christian's advertising agency was growing bigger by the day. He had secured a few major accounts including Chanel. But the stipulation was that I had to do the photography part of the campaign, which I pleasantly accepted. After all, I couldn't very well turn down Christian or Chanel.

A few days had passed and I spent some free time looking at new apartments online. I asked Christian if his realtor had found anything and he told me that he was looking. As I finished the last edits on a new video for my blog and YouTube channel, my phone rang and Christian was calling.

"Hello, handsome."

"Hello, my beautiful girl. What are you doing right now?"

"Nothing. I just finished editing. Why?"

#*Delete*

"Can you meet me somewhere? I want to show you something."

"Sure. Where do you want to meet?"

"113 East 61st Street."

"Okay. I'll leave now."

I ended the call, put on my shoes, and hailed a cab to 113 East 61st Street. When the driver pulled up to the curb, I saw Christian standing there on the sidewalk waiting for me.

"Hello, gorgeous." He smiled as he kissed my lips.

"Hi there." I grinned. "So what did you want to show me?"

He took hold of my hand, led me up five steps to a white building, opened the gorgeous French glass door, and led me inside.

"Wow. This is beautiful. Whose house is this?" I asked.

"I'm hoping it's ours if you like it." He smiled.

"What?" I laughed. "What do you mean 'ours'?"

"I think we should move in together and this would be the perfect house to do that in."

"Are you serious, Christian?"

"I'm very serious, Eloise. I love you and I want to live with you. We practically live together anyway, so we might as well just do it in one house. No more back and forth between our apartments."

"Oh my god. I—yes! I would love to move in together."

"Here?" His brow raised.

"Possibly. Show me the rest of it." I grinned.

He smiled as he took my hand and led me through the six-story townhome.

"It has five bedrooms and five bathrooms," he spoke.

"Do we need that many rooms?" I asked.

"Of course we do. A bedroom for us, two offices and two children."

I stopped dead in my tracks and stared at him, my heart racing with excitement.

"What?" He cocked his head.

"What if I wanted three children?" I smirked.

"Then we'd have to move. No big deal." He shrugged.

I wrapped my arms around his neck and brushed my lips against his.

"I love this place and I love you."

"Good, because I love both of you too."

At that moment, it was a done deal. Christian and I would move in together and start building a life in our new home.

Chapter Forty-Seven

Two Months Later
Christian

Now that Eloise and I were living together in our own home, it was time to take the next step. Her birthday was approaching, so I decided to whisk her away to Chicago for her birthday weekend. What she didn't know was the two surprises I had for her.

"Where are we going?" she asked as we walked down N. Michigan Ave.

"You'll see." I winked as I held on to her hand.

We reached the American Girl store and I opened the door for her.

"Why are we going in here?" She laughed.

"I thought maybe you wanted to buy Maggie a new outfit."

"Really?" She gave me a strange look.

"Yes. Really. To be honest, I'm sick of seeing her always dressed in the same clothes. Brighten her up a little."

We looked at the clothes and Eloise picked out an outfit she liked.

"I'm hungry. Let's go see if we can get some lunch here," I spoke.

"We don't have to eat here. We can go somewhere else. I really don't think this is your thing, Mr. Blake."

"No big deal. Let's just go see if they have any tables available."

I walked her to the Grand Dining Room, where the doors were shut and the hostess was standing outside.

"I was wondering if you had a table for two available?" I asked.

"Of course we do. Follow me."

The moment the doors opened, everyone yelled happy birthday. Eloise cupped her hand over her mouth in shock and then looked at me.

"Christian, what the—"

"Happy birthday, baby." I kissed the side of her head.

****

Eloise

I stood there in shock. I couldn't believe what I saw. My mom, dad, Scarlett, Jeff, Hannah, Claire, Kenny, and Christian's mother and stepfather. Tears filled my eyes as I looked at Christian.

"You threw me an American Girl birthday party?"

"I did." He smiled.

I walked over to the center of the dining room where my

family and friends were standing. All my girls, including my mom and Christian's mom, were holding American Girl dolls. We hugged and some tears were shed, mostly by me.

"Someone else is here to celebrate with you," Christian spoke.

I turned around and he was holding Maggie.

"How did you get her here?"

"I snuck her into my carry-on as you were walking out the front door." He grinned.

I took her from his hands and then hugged him tight.

"Thank you for this. I love you so much."

"You're welcome, baby. I love you too."

We all gathered around the table, ate a delicious lunch, had cake and ice cream, talked, and laughed until we couldn't anymore. Our time was up and we needed to leave the room so they could set up for the next party.

"He's perfect, Eloise." My mom smiled.

"I know he is, Mom."

"He reminds me of your father." She winked.

I gave her a smile and a hug.

"Are you ready, baby?" Christian asked as he placed his hand on the small of my back.

"Yeah. I'm ready. What are we doing next? Is everyone coming?"

"We're going to go explore Chicago and leave the two of you alone," Claire spoke.

"Yeah. I'm sure you have some private celebrating to do after this." Natalie smiled.

"I've booked a dinner reservation for all us at the Skydeck Chicago at eight o'clock. So, we'll see them there," Christian spoke.

We headed back to the hotel, and once we got inside the room, I wasted no time thanking him for everything he'd done for me.

"I can't move." Christian smiled as he looked over at me.

"Me either." I giggled as I snuggled against him.

After a short nap, we showered and dressed for dinner with our family and friends. When we reached the Skydeck, everyone was already there, and I was surprised to see we were the only people in the place.

"You rented out the entire Skydeck again?" I smiled.

"Of course I did. This is a private occasion."

Christian held my hand as we walked over to join our guests.

"I'm not really comfortable up here," Natalie spoke.

"I wasn't at first either, but it's so beautiful."

"I guess." She sighed.

"I can't believe Christian did all this for me and had you all come out here."

"I can." She smiled as she hooked her arm around me. "He's

#Delete

the Prince Charming you've been searching for your whole life."

"I know and I almost blew it."

"No you didn't. He would have never given up on you, and he would have kept on fighting no matter how long it took."

"You think?" I asked with a smile.

"I know."

"Eloise, let's go out on the ledge before dinner," Christian spoke as he walked up behind me.

I hooked my arm in his as he led me to the ledge and we once again stared out at the beautifully lit Chicago city.

"I love you, Eloise," he spoke.

"I love you too, Christian." I smiled at him.

He placed his hand in his pocket and suddenly he got down on one knee.

"Christian, what are you doing?" I began to shake.

"I think you know." He winked. "I have never in my life loved anyone as much as I love you. You complete me, Eloise. From the moment I saw you, I knew I had to make you mine."

"Oh, Christian." The tears started to rise.

"You are the epitome of love and you make my days and my life so much brighter. You are my best friend and my lover, and now, I would love for you to be my wife and spend the rest of your life with me. Eloise, will you marry me?"

"Yes, Christian! Yes, I will marry you!" I exclaimed as the

tears streamed down my face.

He took the two-carat princess cut white gold ring from the box and slipped it on my finger. Then he brought the ring to his lips. Everyone clapped with excitement as he stood up and swung me around.

"I can't believe this!" I cried.

"Believe it, baby, 'cause it happened. We're getting married." He brushed his lips against mine.

"I can't wait to plan this wedding!" Natalie screeched.

We celebrated into the wee hours of the evening and then went back to the hotel and celebrated alone. I couldn't stop staring at the beautiful ring that sat on my finger as my head laid against his chest.

My life was perfect. I was marrying the man of my dreams, my book had hit #1 on the New York Times Bestsellers List, my YouTube channel grew to over two million subscribers, I started doing seminars around the world, Ted Talk, and I was offered my own radio show for an hour three times a week called "Ask Eloise." Now I would move on to the next phase of my life and become Mrs. Christian Blake.

Remember ladies, your Prince Charming is out there, and you'll know it when you first meet him. If you don't have to #Delete him, he's a keeper.

#Delete

Books by Sandi Lynn

If you haven't already done so, please check out my other books. Escape from reality and into the world of romance. I'll take you on a journey of love, pain, heartache and happily ever afters.

Millionaires:
The Forever Series (Forever Black, Forever You, Forever Us, Being Julia, Collin, A Forever Christmas, A Forever Family)
Love, Lust & A Millionaire (Wyatt Brothers, Book 1)
Love, Lust & Liam (Wyatt Brothers, Book 2)
Lie Next To Me (A Millionaire's Love, Book 1)
When I Lie with You (A Millionaire's Love, Book 2)
Then You Happened (Happened Series, Book 1)
Then We Happened (Happened Series, Book 2)
His Proposed Deal
A Love Called Simon
The Seduction of Alex Parker
Something About Lorelei
One Night In London
The Exception
Corporate A$$
A Beautiful Sight
The Negotiation
Defense
Playing The Millionaire

Second Chance Love:
Remembering You
She Writes Love
Love In Between (Love Series, Book 1)
The Upside of Love (Love Series, Book 2)

Sports:
Lightning

About the Author

Sandi Lynn is a New York Times, USA Today and Wall Street Journal bestselling author who spends all her days writing. She published her first novel, Forever Black, in February 2013 and hasn't stopped writing since. Her addictions are shopping, going to the gym, romance novels, coffee, chocolate, margaritas, and giving readers an escape to another world.

Please come connect with her at:

Facebook: www.facebook.com/Sandi.Lynn.Author

Twitter: www.twitter.com/SandilynnWriter

Website: www.authorsandilynn.com

Pinterest: www.pinterest.com/sandilynnWriter

Instagram: www.instagram.com/sandilynnauthor

Goodreads: http://bit.ly/2w6tN25

Printed in Great Britain
by Amazon